Library of Congress Cataloging-in-Publication Data

Bruchac, Joseph, 1942-
  Walking two worlds / Joseph Bruchac.
      pages cm
    ISBN 978-1-939053-13-8 (hardback) -- ISBN 978-1-939053-10-7 (pbk.)
-- ISBN 978-1-939053-96-1 (e-book)
  1. Parker, Ely Samuel, 1828-1895--Childhood and youth--Juvenile fiction.
  [1. Parker, Ely Samuel, 1828-1895--Childhood and youth--Fiction. 2. Seneca
Indians--Fiction. 3. Indians of North America--New York (State)--Fiction. 4.
Education--Fiction. 5. Racism--Fiction.] I. Title.
PZ7.B82816Wal 2015
[Fic]--dc23

                        2014046212

7th Generation
Book Publishing Company
PO Box 99
Summertown, TN 38483
888-260-8458
bookpubco.com

Paperback ISBN: 978-1-939053-10-7
Hardback ISBN: 978-1-939053-13-8

20 19 18 17 16 15   1 2 3 4 5 6 7 8 9

Printed in the United States

Contents

CHAPTER ONE
The White Man Way

Hasanoanda held the plow handle tight.

"Whoa," Hasanoanda shouted. "Stop, Dover."

Dover was the name of the Reverend Stone's stubborn mule. It did not always obey. That was why Hasanoanda had not wrapped the reins around his wrist. He wanted to be able to let go if Dover decided to run.

He did not want to be dragged along behind. That had happened last week to one of the new boys in the Tonawanda Baptist School. That boy's Seneca name was Big Lake. He had been given a new white man name. He was now George. He also now had a sprained wrist.

"Whoa," Hasanoanda shouted again. He pulled harder on the reins. Dover stopped.

Hasanoanda patted the mule on its neck. "You are a good mule," he said in Seneca. He said it in a low voice.

Dover nodded his head as if he understood.

Hasanoanda smiled. "Maybe you are like me," he said. "You do not like to be told what to do in English."

"Eeee-leee," a voice called from the other side of the field. "Ely Parker, come over here."

"You see how it is?" Hasanoanda said to the mule. "Now I must be Ely. 'Hasanoanda' was too hard for Reverend Stone to say. So he gave me his name of Ely." He patted the mule one more time and then ran to the other side of the field.

The reverend Ely Stone was standing next to the boy who was now called George. Elder Stone was a tall man with a long nose. His back was bent like a heron hunting for fish. George was big for his age, but the reverend towered over him. The reverend looked unhappy. George looked even unhappier. He was holding a hoe in his one good hand and staring down at his feet.

"Look what this foolish boy did," Elder Stone said. He pointed his long finger at a mound of dirt. "Do you see that?"

"I see that, sir," Ely said.

The reverend gestured toward George. "Tell him what he did wrong, Ely. You may use Indian to tell him."

"Yes, sir," Ely said. He took the hoe from George's hand. Then Ely used the hoe to level the mound of earth. "We must not plant in hills," he said in Seneca.

George bit his lip. "But that is the way to plant," he said in a soft voice.

Ely shook his head. "No, that is not the white man way. Give me the seeds."

George handed the bag of seeds to Ely. Ely took out several kernels of corn and put them into the ground.

"You see?" Ely said. "This is how white men do it. They just plant corn. They do not mix corn with beans and squash."

George looked confused. "That is strange. Corn and Bean and Squash are Three Sisters. Corn rises up. Bean twines around it. Squash covers the ground and keeps it moist. If you plant them apart, they will not do well."

Ely nodded. "You are right, cousin. The harvest is small when we do it the white man way. But we must do what we are told."

George looked very confused now. "Hasanoanda," he said, "that does not make sense."

Ely nodded again. "I agree. But we must do as we are told. Our parents sent us to this school to learn white man ways. Even when those ways are crazy. Also, do not call me Hasanoanda. You must call me Ely."

Ely turned to Reverend Stone. The reverend was smiling now. "I have told him, sir," Ely said.

Reverend Stone patted him on the shoulder. "Well done, my good and faithful servant," he said.

CHAPTER TWO
Quiet Sounds, Night Sounds

It was dark inside the boys' dormitory room. The girls were in a dormitory room on the other side of the building. The cots in both rooms were small and close to each other. There was only one window. It did not let in much air. It was too hot during the warm moons and too cold in the winter. You could hear everyone else breathing and smell each other's bodies.

The moon shone through the small window near Ely's cot. It reminded him of the story his mother told him. Moon is the grandmother of us all. She looks down on us and worries about us.

Tonight, even the moon could not calm Ely's thoughts. He heard the sad sound of someone crying on the far side of the room.

He knew it was Big Lake, the boy who was now George. Perhaps his sprained wrist was hurting. Perhaps his feelings were hurt. Elder Stone had taken away his name. Then he made him feel foolish.

Ely had cried when he first came to the Tonawanda Baptist School two years ago. He thought of getting up and going over to George. But George was not crying loudly. He did not want sympathy.

"Why are we in such a school?" Ely thought.

But he knew the answer.

If they learned the language and laws of the white man, they might be better able to help their Seneca people. They might be able to defend the little bit of land they had left. The white man had already taken most of their land but still wanted more. The Ogden Land Company was trying to buy their land. The Senecas all said no. They did not want to sell. But the land company kept trying. The land company wanted the Buffalo Creek Reservation land. It wanted the Tonawanda

Reservation land. It wanted the Cattaraugus Reservation land.

George was no longer crying. Perhaps he found peace in his sleep. But Ely could not quiet his own thoughts. He thought about his great-grandfather Handsome Lake, the prophet. He had a great vision and was given the Good Message by the Creator. It came at a time when things were bad for the Six Nations of the Iroquois. After the war between the British and Americans, most of the Iroquois land was taken by the white men. Many Iroquois left their homes and went to Canada. Many Iroquois people began to drink alcohol. Things seemed hopeless.

Handsome Lake's message brought hope. He told them that the Creator wanted them to stop drinking alcohol because it was killing them. He told them it was good to learn some of the white man ways because so many white people were now around them.

Ely thought.

Staring up at the ceiling, he shook his head again. *That is why I am here, but I do not like it. I want to be back home. I want to eat my mother's cooking. I want to help my father, Dragonfly, around our own farm. Our farm is not far away. I could leave and walk home. I'd be home in time for breakfast.*

But he had promised to stay at school. A man must keep his promises.

Ely's thoughts took him back to his parents' farm. He wished his father needed his help, but that was not the case. Two of his two older brothers, Nic and Levi, still lived at home. His mother missed him, but she wanted him to be at school. She wanted it because of her dream.

Ely sat up and looked out the window. His mother's dream. She often told him about it. The dream came to her four months before he was born.

In her dream she was standing near the land of Judge Granger, the Indian agent. It was winter. Heavy snow was falling. The sky was filled with clouds. Suddenly the sky opened. The clouds were swept back by an invisible hand. A rainbow appeared. It reached from the reservation to the Granger farm. That rainbow was broken in the middle of the sky. On the lower side of the rainbow were pictures. They looked like the signs on the little shops in the city.

His parents went to the Dream Speaker the next day.

"You will have a son," he told them. "He will be a peacemaker among our people. He will become a white man with great learning. He will be a warrior for the palefaces. Yet he will never desert his people or lay down his horns as a chief. His name will reach from the sunrise to the sunset, from the winter land to the summer land. His sun will rise on Seneca land and set on white man's land. Yet the ancient land of our people will fold him in when his life ends."

It was still dark outside. The dawn was far away. Tomorrow was another school day.

A dream is a powerful thing. A dream can tell you what to do. *I am supposed to live that dream.*

"I wish my mother never had that dream," Ely whispered.

CHAPTER THREE
Don't Speak Indian

Ely looked out the window. It was a beautiful day. The wind was blowing through the young corn in the school garden. By late summer it would be eight feet tall. Its tassels would be as golden as the hair of the Corn Spirit.

Ely closed his eyes. He saw himself walking through the tall corn.

"Can no one answer this question?" a loud voice said.

Ely opened his eyes. The field of corn was gone. He was sitting at his desk in the school. Reverend Stone was standing at the front of the room. He held a ruler in his right hand as if it were a war club.

"Who will answer my question?" Reverend Stone asked again. He swung the ruler back and forth.

No one answered.

Reverend Stone was not just the Baptist minister. He was also one of their two teachers. The other teacher was his wife.

Mrs. Stone taught the girls sewing, cooking, and housecleaning. Those were the skills needed to be nursemaids and servants in the homes of white people.

Reverend Stone taught reading, writing, and arithmetic. He also supervised the boys in their farm work. The boys did all the farm work. The crops they raised were sold. That brought in more than enough money to pay for their room and board.

All the children were supposed to speak English all the time. They were supposed to speak "Indian" only one day of the week. But when Reverend Stone was not around, they all spoke Seneca.

Ely did not think that Reverend Stone was a good teacher. In church, Reverend Stone was kind to everyone. But in the classroom he was often impatient.

.he reverend walked over to the desk of ᵎ boy named George.

"What is the answer?" he demanded.

George's cheeks grew red. He did not look up or speak.

George had only been in the school for a month. He had not yet learned that white people want you to stare at them when you talk.

Reverend Stone slapped the desk with his ruler.

"LOOK AT ME!"

George raised his head to look at Reverend Stone. George's lips were trembling.

"WHAT . . . IS . . . THE . . . ANSWER?" Reverend Stone shouted.

George took a deep breath. "I . . . I . . . I . . ."

"Foolish boy!" Reverend Stone said. He stepped back and looked around the classroom.

"It is simple subtraction," the reverend said. He picked up a book and shook it at the class. "It is right here in your arithmetic book. What is twelve less eight?"

Ely knew the answer. It came to his mind right away. Four.

Reverend Stone looked around. "Like an owl listening for a mouse," Ely thought.

No one made a sound. It bothered the reverend that his Indian children did not act like white boys and girls. They were never eager to show that they knew the answer first. The reverend liked his Indian students. But he thought they were not very smart. He did not understand how they had been taught at home to help each other and not show off.

Reverend Stone sighed. "Eee-leee! Master Parker," he said. "The answer, please."

"Four," Ely thought again.

But he also thought something else. "Why is English so strange? In Seneca every word always means the same thing. But in English the same sound could mean different things. It could be 'four.' Or 'for.' Or 'fore.'"

The classroom was silent. The other Seneca students were waiting for him to answer, hoping he would give the right answer.

Ely looked into the reverend's eyes. The Seneca way was to look down at the earth when you spoke to an elder. But white men were different. If you did not stare at them, they thought you were ashamed or untrustworthy.

"Four is the answer," Ely said, holding his gaze. He spoke slowly and carefully. He made sure every word was right. "The answer is four, sir."

Reverend Stone clapped his hand on Ely's shoulder. "Excellent. Well said, my boy. Your English is quite good."

Ely knew that was not true. His English was better than the other Seneca students. But his English was not good. If English was a wrestler, it would throw him to the ground.

He wished he could go back to his family's farm. He wished he could leave spelling, grammar, geography, and arithmetic behind. He wished he could be himself again.

Hasanoanda, not Ely.

CHAPTER FOUR
Whirlpool of Words

Ely looked over at his mother and father sitting next to him in the pew. It was Sunday. Sunday was the only day of the week when he could be with his family. They could go to church together at First Baptist Church. Then, after church, he could eat dinner at home before going back to the school.

He looked up at the church ceiling. His father and his older brothers had helped build that ceiling. The church was a fine frame building, so new that Ely could smell the pine boards. It had taken the place of the first church made of logs after Reverend Stone came to Tonawanda thirteen years ago in 1825.

Ely's four brothers and sister sat on his other side—Nic, Levi, Solomon, Newt, and Caroline. All of them were in the front row. The Parkers were a respected family.

Whenever there was any social gathering, Ely's father and mother were there to show their support for the community.

Ely's grandfather Sosehawa was also there. Sosehawa was one of the head chiefs of the Seneca. He was the nephew of Red Jacket, the great orator. The White Father in Washington had admired Red Jacket so much that he gave him a big silver medal. When Red Jacket died, it went to Sosehawa. Today Sosehawa was wearing the Red Jacket medal.

Ely's mother turned her head toward him and smiled.

"Why is she smiling that way?" Ely thought.

Ely looked around the church. Every pew was filled this morning. The service had not yet begun. Going to church was important. Ely's father, Dragonfly, was a church deacon and the church treasurer. He said that what the church taught was good. The church beliefs were like the Seneca beliefs. It was the Seneca way to love your neighbor as yourself. It was the Seneca way to tell the truth. It was the Seneca way not to steal. It was the Seneca way to help the poor. "You can live as a Christian and still be a Seneca," his father had said.

Ely smiled as he remembered something else his father had said: "I think it is harder for white people to live as Christians."

Ely enjoyed church. It was like going to the longhouse in the old days. People came to see each other and be seen. Even some who were not yet Christians came to church.

Everyone wanted to hear what Reverend Stone had to say. He told people what the Bible said. Much of the Bible sounded like the teachings in the Good Message. Some of the old people at Tonawanda said they thought that Jesus Christ must have been an Indian.

Elder Stone's talks were called sermons. Those sermons were in English, a language that most of his congregation could not understand, but there was always a translator. His name was John Hill, a Seneca from Buffalo Creek. His job was to put the preacher's words into Seneca for the congregation.

Ely looked around the room. Where was the translator? He looked up at his mother. That same smile remained on her face. She leaned close to his ear.

"John Hill will not be here today," she whispered. "Today there will be another translator."

Reverend Stone walked into the room. Every face in the congregation turned toward him. He stepped up to the pulpit and nodded at the Parker family in the front pew.

Wolf Woman stood up. "My son will translate today," she said in Seneca. "He can speak the language of the white men perfectly."

The reverend held out a welcoming hand. "Eeee-lee," he said in a warm voice, "Come up here, my son."

Ely opened his mouth. No words came out. Hands pushed him up from his seat. He could not feel his feet as he walked forward. Reverend Stone grasped him by the shoulder and turned him to face the congregation.

A hymn was being sung by everyone in Seneca. It was a long song with many choruses. Ely was glad of that. He did not have to say anything while everyone sang. But that hymn ended too quickly.

The reverend began to speak. Everyone was looking at them. Ely strained to hear Elder Stone's words. A strange thing began to happen. The faces of the congregation blurred. The air felt thick. Ely felt like he was underwater.

Reverend Stone paused. It was Ely's turn. He did not have to speak English; he just had to say words in Seneca. But the English words were like a whirlpool twisting his thoughts around.

Ely closed his eyes. He tried to speak. It was like spitting out a mouthful of cotton.

"Klist," he said, "wants … us … to … to … "

The whirlpool in his head was getting larger. Things were spinning all around him.

Then everything went black.

"You will do better," Wolf Woman said as they left the church. She brushed back the hair from Ely's forehead to look at the bump there. It was still swelling. Ely's head had struck the floor when he fainted and fell forward.

His brothers and his sister had gone on ahead.

"Yes. You will do better," his mother repeated.

Dragonfly, who was walking by Ely's other side, said nothing.

When they reached their home, Ely's mother went inside. His father put out one hand. Ely stopped.

His father sat down on the steps. Ely sat next to him. They sat together for a while. Neither of them said anything.

Then Dragonfly put his hand on Ely's shoulder and gently squeezed it.

"Hasanoanda, my son," he said. "You need to get a different education. You must go to Grand River."

CHAPTER FIVE
A New Adventure

Ely turned toward his father. "Grand River?" he said. "Grand River!"

His father nodded.

"Yes. You can go to the home of my older cousin, Hummingbird, and his wife Near the Sky. They will be happy to have you stay with them. Their children are grown and have moved away."

Grand River! Ely felt excited.

Grand River was the big Indian reserve in Canada. Joseph Brant, the Mohawk war leader, was awarded the land by the British for his loyalty during the American Revolution. Brant invited all the people of the Six Nations to join him. Many Mohawks, Senecas, Onondagas, Oneidas, Cayugas, and Tuscaroras followed him to Canada. But many stayed in New York.

"What is it like at Grand River?" Ely asked his father.

"Different from here," Dragonfly said. There was a little smile on his face. He was teasing his son.

"Father!" Ely said. "Tell me."

Dragonfly chuckled. "It is better in some ways. It is not surrounded by white people trying to take the land. The forests have not all been turned into farms. All the game animals have not been killed by white hunters."

"What will I do there?" Ely said. "Will I go to school?"

Dragonfly shook his head. "There is a schoolhouse there and many of our people there live in big houses like white people. But your uncle and aunt do not live that way. Hummingbird hunts and fishes and traps. That is part of what he can teach you."

This was the old Seneca way. At a certain age, a boy would go to stay with his uncle. A boy could learn more from an uncle than a father. The father might know the same things, but the boy would learn better from the uncle.

"I will like that," Ely said.

"I know you will," Dragonfly said.

"Yes," Ely said. Then the smile left his face. "What about my mother? She wants me to learn to be a white man. I cannot leave if she does not agree."

Dragonfly nodded.

"I have already spoken with her. Your mother agrees. You must learn the ways of the white men, but you must also know our old ways. Grand River is the place for you to do that."

"How long will I stay there?" Ely asked.

"Until you are ready to come home."

"When will I go?"

Dragonfly squeezed his son's shoulder. "Chief Blacksmith is leaving tomorrow for a meeting with the Six Nations chiefs. He does not speak any English. He may need to talk to white people along the way. You can translate for him."

Ely looked uncertain. "Are you sure I can do that?"

Dragonfly smiled. "Yes," he said. Then he poked his son in the ribs with his finger. "It will be easy for you to put his words into English. It will not be like trying to turn our preacher's words into Seneca."

Ely laughed. His father's teasing was always gentle. It never made him feel foolish.

As his father stood to climb the steps, Ely thought of something.

"Father?" he said.

Dragonfly turned around. "What is it?"

"If it is so good at Grand River, why did so many stay here?"

"We stay," Dragonfly said, "because this is our home."

CHAPTER SIX
Chief Blacksmith

Early the next morning, Ely and his father left their farm. The sun was not yet up. It was late spring and already warm. It was best to start out on a journey before the heat of the day. Chief Blacksmith and two other Seneca men were already waiting at the crossroads. The two others were chief Isaac Shanks and his cousin Dragging Horns. Like Chief Blacksmith, they could not speak English.

Chief Blacksmith was a dignified older man, the leading chief of the Senecas. He carried the title of Donehogawa, Keeper of the Western Door.

"I greet you in peace, my friends," Dragonfly and Ely said.

"I greet you in peace," the three men replied.

"I hope you have not waited long for us," Dragonfly said.

"Not that long," Chief Blacksmith said in his deep voice. "Although I was only a young boy when I first got here."

"Ah," Dragonfly said. "I believe that." He pointed at Ely with his chin. "When we left home this morning, my son here was just this tall." He held his hand down by his knee. "Look at him now!"

Ely smiled at their joking. It was often that way when respected Seneca leaders got together. They did not behave like important white men who always acted so serious.

Chief Blacksmith turned to Ely. "So this is Hasanoanda."

"Yes," Dragonfly said. "He can help you."

Chief Blacksmith nodded. "I am sure he will be helpful. I have heard that he is a fine young man." He looked at Ely. "So, you wish to go to Grand River?"

Ely nodded, looking politely down at the ground.

"Do you speak English well?"

Ely shook his head. "I speak it. But I do not speak it well."

Chief Blacksmith laughed. His laugh came from deep in his chest like the rumble of thunder. "Good," he said. "Hasanoanda, I like it that you are honest. But I am sure you will do well. We will not ask you to translate any sermons."

Ely laughed in spite of himself. The chief's sense of humor was like that of Ely's father. "It will be easy to travel with him," Ely thought.

Ely's father put his arms around him. Ely leaned his head on his father's broad chest. He was eager to go to Grand River. But now he felt sad that he was leaving home. Dragonfly let go of him and stepped back. He handed his son a pack that held clothing and food for the journey. Then he walked away. He did not look back over his shoulder.

That was the Seneca way. When someone left, you did not say good-bye. White men did that. There was no word for "good-bye" in Seneca.

"Hasanoanda," Chief Blacksmith said. "Let's go."

CHAPTER SEVEN
Two Bits Is Twenty-Five Cents

The journey to Grand River was only about ninety miles, as white men measured it. As the Senecas measured it, it was a journey of three sleeps.

The roads and trails were level and easy to walk. They spent their first night in the home of a Seneca family on the American side of the Niagara River.

The next morning they came to the ferry that crossed the river. Blacksmith gestured to Ely.

"Hasanoanda," he said. "Talk to the American who runs this ferry. If we only speak Seneca, he may try to cheat us." Blacksmith gave Ely several coins. "Pay him with this."

The white man standing next to his ferry was chewing tobacco. He was short and skinny. He wore a black hat pulled down tight on his head. The hat made his big ears stick out to the side.

"If this man was a Seneca," Ely thought, "he would be called Ears Like Wings." He walked up to the man.

"Good morning, sir," he said in his best English.

The man looked surprised. "You speak American?" he said.

"Yes," Ely nodded. "We . . ." He looked at the ferry, which was little more than a raft. "We . . . cross."

A crafty look came over the man's face. "Want to get across, eh? Well, there's four of you. Ayup, one, two, three, four. So I calculate that you owes me four bits."

Four bits? Two bits was twenty-five cents. Four bits was fifty cents. Ely looked at the signboard next to the ferry. It listed the rates for crossing. A horse and wagon with two passengers was twenty-five cents. A single person was six cents. They had no horse or wagon. The man was trying to cheat them.

Ely walked over to the signboard and pointed at it. He forced himself to look the ferryman straight in the eye.

"Sir," he said in a polite voice. "You mean two bits? Six times four equals twenty-four. Plus one cent for tip?"

The ferryman looked confused.

"I'll be danged," the skinny white man said to himself.

"He's never met an Indian who can read and multiply," Ely thought. That thought almost made him laugh. But he kept a serious look on his face.

"Sir?" Ely said. He counted out twenty-five cents. "Here."

The ferryman took the twenty-five cents.

None of them spoke while they were crossing. When they reached the other side, they got off and walked until the ferry was out of sight.

Then Chief Blacksmith took Ely's hand and shook it.

"Hasanoanda," Chief Blacksmith said, grinning broadly. "You did well."

CHAPTER EIGHT
A Traditional Home

When they reached Grand River, Ely thought that the three older men would leave him. They were expected at the council house.

"I know your aunt and uncle," Chief Shanks said. "I will show you to the cabin of Near the Sky."

So the three men went with Ely to the cabin of Near the Sky and Hummingbird. The two old people were standing in front of the cabin. Hummingbird was a tall, thin man. His face was long and his smile was pleasant. He was much older than Ely's father, but he still looked strong. He moved gracefully. Near the Sky was short and round. When she smiled, her wrinkled face looked as bright as the sun. She was not graceful like her husband. She seemed to bounce around like a ball.

"I am going to like being here," Ely thought.

He could smell something cooking.

Everyone greeted each other. Near the Sky pointed with her chin behind the cabin. There was a fire there with a pot hung over it and logs to sit on around the fire circle.

"Let us eat some food." Near the Sky said. Her voice was friendly and pleasant to hear.

That was the Seneca way. Visitors were always given food. You had to accept, whether you were hungry or not.

Ely was very hungry. He felt like running to that food. But he let the older men walk ahead of him.

As they passed behind the house, Ely saw many things there. Fish traps woven from willow branches. Animal skins tied onto stretching hoops. A beautiful birch bark canoe turned upside down with two carved paddles leaning against it.

Everyone except Hummingbird sat down on the logs around the fire. The stew in the pot smelled so good that Ely's mouth was watering.

"Creator," Hummingbird said, raising his arms. "We are grateful for this gift of food. We thank you. We thank my wife for cooking it so well."

"Nya:weh," everyone said.

Hummingbird sat and they all began to eat. They did not use plates. Every Seneca always carried a wooden spoon hung from his or her belt. They all dipped into the pot of venison stew. It seemed to be the best food Ely had ever tasted.

When they were done, everyone stood.

"Nya:weh," Chief Blacksmith said. "We all thank you for this good food."

He put his hands on Ely's shoulders. "Your nephew is a good young man," Chief Blacksmith said. "I would be glad to travel with him again."

CHAPTER NINE
First Morning

There was no bedroom for Ely. He slept by the fireplace wrapped in a blanket. His aunt and uncle were in the small loft above. There was just enough room up there for the two of them. To get up to that loft they climbed a log with notches cut into it.

Ely did not mind sleeping on the plank floor by the fire. He often chose to sleep that way at home. He liked the warmth of the fire and the sound of the logs burning.

There was a pile of dry, split wood by the fire. "I will add more to the fire when it burns down," he thought. He covered his head with the blanket.

When he woke, it was early morning. Birds were singing outside. The fire was still burning. He had slept through the night, but either his uncle or his aunt had added more wood without waking him.

"Hasanoanda," Near the Sky called from outside. Her voice was as musical as the singing birds. "Come here, nephew."

Ely unwrapped himself from the wool blanket. He hugged himself and rubbed his arms. Then he pulled on his pants and his shirt. His clothes were cold from being left on the floor all night. The plank floor was also cold as he crossed it on his bare feet. He sat on a bench to pull on his socks and his shoes. Then, rubbing his eyes, he stepped outside.

His aunt and his uncle were waiting for him. His uncle was wearing a light wool shirt, deerskin leggings, and moccasins. His long gray hair was parted in the middle and tied into two braids. He had a small pack on his back. His aunt wore a long skirt and a blouse. She had a red Hudson's Bay blanket around her shoulders. She was holding a leather pouch.

"Did you sleep well?" his aunt asked in her musical voice.

"Yes," Ely said. "I slept well. A baby could not sleep better than I slept."

A smile came to his uncle's long face.

"Good," his uncle said. He leaned down toward Ely. "Did you dream?"

Ely shook his head. "Not last night."

"Ah," his uncle said. "Will you tell me when you do dream?"

Ely understood. Dreams often were messages. Sometimes they told you what your heart wanted you to do. Other times, dreams came from the natural world or the Creator. They might even predict the future.

Like his mother's strange dream? Had it really predicted how his own life would be? Ely pushed that thought away. His uncle was still waiting for an answer.

Ely nodded. "Yes, my uncle," he said. "I will tell you my dreams."

"Good," Hummingbird said. "Now I will tell you my dream. In my dream I took you into the woods and left you there."

His uncle pointed with his chin at the woods that came close to the back of the cabin. "Let's go."

He turned gracefully and began to walk toward the forest. Ely's aunt pushed the leather pouch she was holding into Ely's hands.

"Tie this to your belt," she said. "Cornmeal."

Ely stood there for a moment. He was barely awake. He felt confused.

Near the Sky took off the Hudson's Bay blanket, put it over Ely's shoulders, and gave him a gentle push.

"Go," she said.

CHAPTER TEN

Deep in the Forest

Ely thought he knew how to move quietly through the woods. But Ely soon saw that his uncle knew much more than he did. His uncle was twice as big as he was, but he was also twice as quiet.

At Tonawanda the forests were not large. White men had cut down all the trees around their reservation. The forest around Grand River seemed to have no end. They started off on a trail but soon turned off it. They pushed through brush, ducked under tree branches, crawled over fallen trees. They climbed up and down hills, crossed swampy places, and jumped over little streams.

Ely's shoes felt heavy on his feet and his wool socks were wet. He tripped often and stepped on dead branches that cracked under his weight. Dry leaves rustled under his feet, and he caught his sleeves on branches. A blackberry cane scratched his cheek.

He was used to walking, but this walk through the forest was tiring him out. His uncle, though, passed easily through the brush and berry bushes. The hemlock and spruce branches seemed to move aside to make way for him. He passed through the woods like a fish through water.

They only paused once. That was when they came to a swamp. Many cattail plants grew in that swamp. Some had dried stalks with bundles of fluff on top. Hummingbird looked at the cattail plants and then at Ely. Ely understood. He gathered several handfuls of the dry, cottony fluff and placed them in the pouch that hung on his belt. He would use it later when he started a campfire.

Hummingbird started walking again. His uncle was a swift walker. Ely's legs were much shorter than his uncle's. But Ely was determined. On he walked. On and on.

Ely looked up at the clear sky as they began to climb a hill. The sun was three hands high. By a white man's watch, it would be about ten o'clock. Ely shook his head. A watch was no use here in the woods. He was not in school where lives were ruled by a clock. White man's time did not live here.

His uncle stopped in a clear space near the top of the hill. A big rock ledge leaned out from the hillside. Ely was breathing hard as he caught up to his uncle. His uncle did not look tired at all. Ely's heart was pounding and he was sweating. But he had kept up.

The two of them stood there for a while. All Ely could see was forest. It seemed to go on forever.

"The trees here are so big," Ely said. "It is good."

Hummingbird nodded. "Here some of us can still live in something like the old way." He looked toward the east. "But over that way are cities of white men. Hamilton. Toronto. Even here in Canada they make their towns bigger, clear land for farms, build more roads." He turned back and looked out again over the valley. "However, this is still here. We hope it will always be here."

Hummingbird plucked a blackberry leaf from Ely's hair.

"You walked well through the forest, nephew," he said.

Ely shook his head. "I made more noise than a blind bear with three legs."

Hummingbird let out a loud laugh. It echoed back from the hills on the other side of the valley below. He shook his head.

"I did not say you were quiet, nephew. I said you walked well. You kept up and did not stop. You have a strong will. That is not something I can teach you. However, I can teach you to walk more quietly."

He looked at Ely's feet. "But not in those heavy shoes. Take those off."

Ely sat down and removed his shoes and socks.

Hummingbird pulled the pack from his shoulders and took out a pair of moccasins. He put Ely's shoes and socks into his pack.

Ely slid the moccasins on. They fit his bare feet perfectly. Even without socks, they felt warmer than his shoes.

"Here," his uncle said.

Ely looked up. Hummingbird was holding something out. It was a shard of flint and a small, curved piece of steel.

"You know how to use these?"

Ely took the flint in one hand and the steel in the other. He struck the two together and made a spark fly.

"Good," Hummingbird said. "Make a fire to stay warm through the night. There is much dead wood here that you can gather." He looked down the hill. "There is a spring down there." He took a sheathed knife from his pack. "Use this to cut hemlock boughs for a lean-to."

He looked toward the rock face. "Make your shelter there. The rock will block the north wind."

Ely nodded. He felt nervous but made his face stay calm.

"Stay here," his uncle said. "I will be back."

Hummingbird began to walk away.

"Uncle," Ely said.

Hummingbird looked back over his shoulder.

"When will you be back?" Ely asked.

Hummingbird's face split into that wide grin of his. "When you see me again."

CHAPTER ELEVEN
Mosquitoes

Ely listened. He had always been a good listener. He liked listening to his father and mother tell stories of long ago. He liked listening to the long conversations that visitors had around the fire in the Parker house.

But this was a different kind of listening. At his home in Tonawanda, there were people talking. There were the noises from their farm animals out back. Even at night one might hear the sounds of wagons passing on the road.

He was now far away from people, any noisy chickens and pigs, and roads. All he could hear was the sound of wind moving through the trees. Each tree turned the wind into a different sound. The soft needles of the pines whispered. The hard leaves of the beech trees rattled. Ely had heard such sounds from the trees before, but never for this long. It was like music.

Then he heard something else. Feet moving loudly through the leaves. Coming his way. Making as much noise as a big clumsy person would make. A white man might think it was a moose or a bear.

Ely was sure he knew what was making that sound.

Closer and closer it came. Then, only a few feet away, the one that made all that noise appeared. A chipmunk! Ely smiled. Sometimes the smallest ones made the most noise. Ely had never seen a bear or a moose. But his father had told him that such big animals make less noise in the forest than the squirrels and chipmunks.

Ely did not move. The chipmunk ran up, touched Ely's leg with its nose, and darted back into the leaves.

After that, the sounds from the forest increased. A wood thrush sang. A red squirrel chirred from a treetop. A red-headed woodpecker pounded a hollow beech tree.

The sun moved farther across the sky. Ely heard a faint noise off to his right. He turned his eyes that way. A big tom turkey stuck its head out from behind a tree. Its long beard hung down below its chin. It bobbed its head back and forth. Six smaller turkeys followed it. They looked like bent old people wrapped in feather blankets. They pecked at the ground as they took slow, careful steps, paying no attention to Ely. They strutted past him back into the forest.

Something growled. Was that a bear? Then Ely realized it was his stomach.

He cleared away the leaves and twigs from the ground in front of him. He gathered stones and placed them in a circle. He found one flat rock the size of a plate and leaned it against his fire circle.

He walked downhill and found the spring Hummingbird told him about flowing out of the hillside. There was a small pool of water beneath it. Ely knelt and let the sweet water fill his mouth. Drinking water made his stomach stop growling. However, he was still hungry.

He looked around. There was a birch tree with loose bark.

"My friend," he said. "I am going to take part of your blanket. Thank you for giving it to me."

Ely took his knife and carefully peeled off a foot-wide piece of birch bark. He removed his knife from the sheath and trimmed the edges of the quarter-inch-thick piece of bark. He cut a long, green twig from a maple and chopped the twig into four pieces, each one the size of a four-inch nail. He folded in the corners of the birch bark and pierced each of the corners with a piece of twig to hold the corners in place.

Ely held up what he had made. It was not as good as the bark baskets his mother made. But it was good enough. It would hold as much as a metal pail. He felt pleased with himself. This first night alone in the forest would be easy.

But as he held up his birch bucket he heard a new sound. Something buzzed around his head. A mosquito had found him.

He had forgotten about mosquitoes. That mosquito would be the first of many. He had heard that there were more mosquitoes here than at Tonawanda.

The sun was only two hands above the trees. Clouds of mosquitoes would come when it got dark. He remembered the story Wolf Woman told about the giant mosquito that lived long ago. It was so big it would drain people of all their blood. A brave hunter managed to kill that giant mosquito. But then people made the mistake of trying to get rid of its huge body by burning it. Thick smoke rose from its body and turned into mosquitoes. To this day, those children of the giant mosquito still drain the blood from our bodies.

Ely knew he would have to work quickly.

He reached down into the pool of water and scraped a handful of sandy mud from the bottom. Ely wiped that mud on his arms and ankles, around his neck, and on his face. It would be much better if the mud had clay in it. Clay sticks to the skin better than sand. It would be even better if he had bear grease. Bear grease protects your skin from insect bites. But this sandy mud would have to do.

He filled his bucket with water and walked back up the hill with it. He placed it next to the circle of stones.

What now? Make a lean-to? Make his fire? He looked up at the sky. No clouds. The air felt dry. There was no longer any wind. It was not going to rain anytime soon. Making shelter could wait.

The stack of dry wood he'd gathered should be enough to last the night. Ely made a pile of dry twigs from the pines, small strips of birch bark, and an old bird's nest that he found on the ground. The pile looked like a little conical wigwam. In the center of that conical wigwam he put a handful of the cattail fluff he saved earlier in the day.

More mosquitoes were beginning to fly around his head. It was getting darker. Those mosquitoes were not biting him yet. The dry mud was protecting him. But he knew it would not be enough.

Ely took out the flint and steel. He struck the flint with the steel. A spark leaped out and fell just short of the tinder. He struck again. The second spark landed on the edge of the bird's nest. It glowed and then went out. As he struck a third spark, a mosquito bit him on the eyelid. It made his hand jump and he missed again. Ely took a deep breath.

Do not hurry. When you hurry, things go wrong.

The fourth spark fell into the middle of the cattail fluff.

Ely placed his hands on the ground and put his head close to the pile of twigs and bark. A mosquito was biting him on his ear. He ignored it. He blew a slow and steady breath. As he blew, the spark grew stronger. The cattail fluff smoked and glowed red near that spark. Ely blew again. Thick white smoke rose up. He blew a third time and a fourth, turning his head away between breaths. On his fourth breath, flames shot up. They crackled as the fire caught the birch bark and pine twigs.

Ely carefully added larger sticks. Soon his fire was burning strong.

He adjusted the flat stone within the fire circle. The flames reflected off the surface of the flat stone. He poured cornmeal into his hand and dripped water into it. He mixed it into a ball. It made a hissing sound as he flattened it onto the hot stone. With his knife, he turned the cake until it was brown on both sides. He lifted it with the knife blade and his fingertips, and moved it back and forth between his palms to cool it. Then he took a bite. His aunt had added sugar to the corn meal. It tasted sweet and wonderful.

It was dark all around. But he had fire and food. The mosquitoes were no longer biting. Ely leaned back against the stone ledge with a smile on his face.

CHAPTER TWELVE
The Visitor

Ely opened his eyes. It was still dark all around. He'd woken twice before to put wood on the fire. This time was different. He felt he was being watched. He looked around. At first all he saw was the fire. Then he saw them. Two eyes in the darkness reflecting back the firelight.

The eyes moved closer. Now Ely could see the shape of a head, then a body. A big dog? No, a black wolf!

The black wolf walked forward until it almost reached the fire, then it sat down. It kept looking at him.

"This must be a dream," Ely thought.

"I greet you in peace, clan brother," Ely said in a soft voice. "I am a wolf, too."

The black wolf just sat there.

"What a good dream this is," Ely thought. He closed his eyes.

When he opened them again it was morning. His fire had burned to ashes. The mosquitoes had come back when the fire went out. His face was covered with bumps from their bites.

His uncle, Hummingbird, was sitting next to him.

Hummingbird handed him a small bottle. Ely pulled out the cork to smell it. Salve. His mother made the same salve from medicine plants. He rubbed the salve on the insect bites and they stopped itching.

Hummingbird held out a piece of flat, dry fungus. Ely had seen it growing on the birch trees.

"Next time," Hummingbird said, "put this on the coals. The smoke keeps away the mosquitoes."

Ely began to make sure the fire was out when he remembered the wolf.

"I had a dream," he said.

"A dream?" Hummingbird said. "About a wolf?"

"Yes," Ely replied. "How did you know?"

Hummingbird pointed with his chin to the other side of the fire.

There in the soft earth were the paw prints of a huge wolf. Ely took a deep breath and a smile came to his face.

Hummingbird waited while Ely ran his hands through the ashes to make sure the fire was out, took apart the fire circle, and put the stones back where they had been. When Ely was done, Hummingbird nodded his head.

"My brother taught you well," he said.

"Thank you, uncle," he said. "But I have more to learn."

"That is very true," Hummingbird agreed. That made them both smile.

As they walked back through the forest, neither of them spoke. Finally, when they reached the edge of the woods, Ely said, "Uncle, a wolf came and visited me. It was not a dream."

"Yes," Hummingbird said.

"What does it mean?'

"It means that a wolf came and visited you."

CHAPTER THIRTEEN
Family Embrace

The days went by quickly. Ely thought about the black wolf. He did not see it again, but at times he felt as if it was watching over him. He felt as if it had brought him a message from his mother.

His mother's name was Wolf Woman. Her clan was the Wolf Clan. Since a clan was inherited from a person's mother, that made Ely part of the Wolf Clan too. Wolf Clan people were often like the wolf. They were swift-moving scouts who would venture far out on their own.

Ely followed his uncle into the forest each day. He learned how to make a birch bark canoe and fish at night while holding a torch. He learned how to choose the right deer to hunt. Not a doe with fawns or a big buck leading the herd. The right deer to hunt was one that was fat and did not have fawns.

Sometimes Hummingbird went to the trading post. He brought in the skins of the animals he and Ely trapped. He exchanged them for such things as flour, sugar, and ammunition. Ely went along on those trips to the trading post. He helped carry the skins and made sure the trader added everything up right.

There were young people of Ely's age at Grand River. He made friends with some of them. When they played games of lacrosse, Ely took part. He was a swift runner. Everyone wanted him on their team. He also was a strong wrestler. No one could throw him to the ground. He even beat boys who were much taller and heavier.

Some of his new friends attended school. The church school at Grand River was much bigger than the Baptist school on his reservation. But Ely did not go to that white man's school at Grand River. He was not interested in that kind of learning.

Spring returned to the woods. New leaves grew on the trees. A year had passed. Ely was two fingers taller than when he first came to Grand River.

At the end of that year, Ely traveled back home. His mother was sitting on the porch of their cabin. Somehow she knew he was coming. It was always that way with his mother.

She stepped down from the porch and wrapped her arms around him.

"You are so big," Wolf Woman said. "They fed you well."

"Their food is not as good as yours, my mother," Ely said.

Wolf Woman hugged him again. "I missed you," she whispered in his ear. There were tears in her eyes.

Ely nodded. There were tears in his eyes as he looked around. Where was everyone else? As always, his mother knew what he was thinking.

"Your father has gone to town. Your two little brothers are with him. Nic and Caroline are at school. They began to study there this year." She looked into Ely's eyes.

"Are you home now to stay?" his mother asked.

Ely shook his head. He thought of the black wolf. "I must learn more of our old ways," he said. "I need to understand what it was to be a Seneca before everything changed."

His mother nodded. "I see," she said.

They heard the sound of a wagon approaching.

"Go," Wolf Woman said. "Greet your father and your little brothers."

There was a big smile on Newt's face when he saw Ely. He raised his hand in greeting.

Ely did not have time to wave back. Little Solomon had leaped from the wagon bed and was running toward Ely as fast as he could.

"Hasanoanda, my brother!" Solomon shouted. "You are back. You are back."

He leaped up into Ely's arms, almost knocking him down. A pair of arms wrapped around

Ely as Newt reached them. Then Dragonfly's huge arms embraced all three of them.

"My son," Dragonfly said. "We missed you."

Later that day, Ely walked with his father around the farm.

"My son," Dragonfly said, "have you learned enough from my brother?"

Ely shook his head. "There is more that I want to learn."

Dragonfly leaned back against a rail fence. "Knowing our old ways will make you stronger. They will help you to always remember who you are."

Dragonfly knelt and picked up a handful of soil. "You will not forget that we belong to this land. You will not sign it away."

Ely noticed the sad look on his father's face.

"What happened while I was gone?" Ely asked.

"The Ogden Land Company tricked some of our men into getting drunk. They made them sign a paper. Those men were not chiefs. They had no right to sell the land.

But the land company took that paper to the white man court. They said it proved that the Ogden Land Company now owned all of Tonawanda."

Dragonfly poured the soil from his hand. He patted it gently.

"Our chiefs have gone to Albany," he said. "We are not giving up this land." Then he looked up at Ely. "You have grown taller. Your shoulders are broader. That is good. There will be much weight for you to carry. We will all need your help one day."

Ely nodded his head. His father's words touched his heart and made him wonder what he could do.

"Should I stay here?" Ely asked. "Not go back to Grand River?

Dragonfly shook his head. "No. For now, follow your heart. You will know when it is time to come back home."

The next day was a Sunday. At the Baptist Church, Ely sat between Nic and Caroline. Caroline held his hand all through the service.

"We miss you at our school, Master Parker," Reverend Stone said after the service. "I have prayed for your return."

Ely nodded. "Thank you, sir."

Other Seneca boys and girls came up to greet him. Ely had not realized he was so well liked. But one boy was missing.

"Where is Big Lake?"

"Who is that?" Nic said.

"What was his English name?" Caroline said.

"George," Ely said. "They called him George."

Nic sighed. "Oh," he said. He looked down at the ground. "He is gone."

"Is he at his home?" Ely asked.

Nic shook his head. "His father was one of those men who signed the paper that sold our land. He was so ashamed of himself that he threw a bottle of whiskey into the fire. That set their whole cabin on fire. George was able to save his little sisters and his mother. When he went back in to get his father, the roof fell on them."

They walked on in silence. Ely thought about George and everything else happening at Tonawanda. Too many sad things. He had missed his parents, his brothers, and his sister. But now all he wanted was to go back to Grand River.

Nic reached into his pocket and took out a stone. He handed it to Ely. The stone had a hole in the middle of it. Ely held up it up and looked through the hole. A stone such as this was special.

He tried to give it back to Nic.

"Keep it, brother," Nic said.

Ely closed his fingers around the stone. He felt it grow warm in his hand. "Nya:weh," he said.

"It would be good to have you with us in school," Nic said.

Ely nodded. "Someday," he said. "Not now."

"Could you write to us?" Caroline asked. "I am learning how to write letters."

Ely liked the idea of getting letters from his sister. But his own English was not good enough to write.

"No," he said. He held up the stone. "I will look through this and see you."

CHAPTER FOURTEEN
Ways of the Warrior

Ely returned to Grand River.

His education continued. He gained blisters and skill using a bow and arrow. He learned how to draw back the bowstring and quickly release the arrow. Before long, he could strike things thrown high in the air. One day, Hummingbird brought out a long object wrapped in leather. It was a gun.

"I fought in two wars for the British," Hummingbird said. "I learned how to use this. Now you will learn."

Hummingbird leaned a board against a tree. He took out a powder horn and poured gunpowder into the gun barrel. Then he dropped in a lead bullet followed by a piece of cloth for wadding. He pulled out the long steel ramrod and pushed it into the barrel to tamp everything down.

His uncle raised the gun to his shoulder.

BAM!

The board jumped. Hummingbird had hit it in the center.

"Your turn," Hummingbird said.

Ely picked up the gun. It was heavy in his hands. As he tried to pour the gunpowder down the barrel, some of it spilled. Ely bent to pick up the spilled gunpowder.

Hummingbird shook his head. "There will be dirt in it. Leave it there."

Ely tried again. He poured gunpowder down the long barrel. He dropped in a lead ball. He picked up the ramrod. Then he saw how his uncle was looking at him.

"Oh," Ely said. "I almost forgot the wadding."

Hummingbird smiled.

Soon the gun was loaded. Ely looked at his uncle. Dragonfly nodded. Ely lifted the gun and pointed it at the board. He pulled the trigger.

BOOM!

The butt of the muzzle-loader slammed back into Ely's shoulder. The sound of the gunshot was very loud. The bullet hit the tree three feet above the board.

Ely lowered the gun and rubbed his right shoulder.

"Good," Hummingbird said. "Your gun just taught you three lessons. First, do not put in too much gunpowder. Second, a gun kicks back. Hold it firm against your shoulder so it does not hurt you. Third, do not hurry."

In a battle, his uncle told him, most men miss their target because they shoot over the heads of the enemy.

"One slow, careful shot is better than a hundred fast ones."

Ely was glad to learn about guns from his uncle. The Seneca nation would never again fight the white men. They had made that promise to President Washington. But his mother had dreamed that he would be a warrior. Learning about guns was part of being a warrior.

That second year passed even more quickly than the first. Ely still enjoyed learning from his uncle, but he thought often of home. He worried about the Ogden Land Company taking away their land. He remembered what his father had said to him. He would know when it was time to return home.

Ely held up the stone with a hole in it. He looked through it. He thought about his family. *I want to see the faces of my parents, my brothers, and my sister. I have learned enough here.*

He went to his aunt and uncle.

"I thank you for all you have given me," he said. "But my heart misses my home."

"Then you must go," Near the Sky said.

CHAPTER FIFTEEN
"Hello, Young Savage"

"Hasanoanda," a voice whispered close to Ely's ear. "Hasanoanda." A hand gently shook his shoulder.

His aunt, Near the Sky, was leaning over him. Back home at Tonawanda, Ely had always been the first to rise. But here at Grand River, hard as he tried, his aunt and uncle always woke up before him.

It was still dark outside. But the fireplace cast enough light for him to look around the room. He could see the others wrapped in their blankets around him on the floor. The four Mohawk men who had come to visit were still sleeping. Hummingbird and Near the Sky were known for their hospitality. Any traveler was welcome to share their food and spend the night.

"He is waiting," Near the Sky said.

Ely had slept with his clothes on. He pulled on his moccasins and stood up.

"Thank you," he said. "Thank you for everything."

Near the Sky handed him a bag of food for his journey. It felt warm and smelled like corn cakes sweetened with maple sugar.

His aunt gave him a little push. "Go," she said. "Travel safely." She stayed by the fireplace as he walked away.

He stepped carefully around the sleeping men as he crossed the room. Then he paused by the door to pull back his long hair and tie it into a ponytail. Hummingbird was standing outside. His breath formed white clouds around his face. The spring morning was cold, but he wore no coat. Neither did Ely.

Ely took a deep breath of the good morning air. Then he took his uncle's hand. They did not shake as white men do. They grasped each other's hands gently.

"I will not forget," Ely said.

"We know," Hummingbird said. He let go of Ely's hand and went back into the cabin.

As he began his journey home, Ely followed the same road he had taken before. On the second day, as he reached a crossroads on the edge of the Canadian city called London, a voice called to him.

"Hello, young savage!"

Ely turned. He saw a group of four young white men. There were smiles on all their faces. One of them was waving at him. They were very well dressed in the same kind of red clothing. There was a word for that kind of clothing. Uniforms. That was it. Such uniforms meant they were soldiers.

"Hello," Ely replied in English.

The four young men seemed surprised. The tallest of the four men looked at the one who had waved at Ely.

"Dennis, my man," he said. "Have you found us an educated savage?"

"Let me see," the young man named Dennis said. He turned toward Ely and held out his hand.

"Pleased to meet you," Dennis said.

Ely took Dennis's hand and looked him in the eye.

"Pleased," Ely said slowly, "Pleased . . . to . . . meet . . . you."

It had been a long time since Ely spoke English. But he thought he said the words well. However, for some reason, all four of the white soldiers laughed.

"A wonder!" the tallest of the soldiers said.

"A parrot," said the shortest of the four. "The lad is just saying what you said. He's like a silly bird taught to make sounds."

Dennis made a gesture toward the short soldier. "Ralph," he said, "hold on. Let me test our new . . . friend."

He turned back toward Ely again.

"My name is lieutenant Dennis James Cross of Derby, England. Dennis, for short. This rough lot behind me are my fellow officers."

Ely nodded. The young soldier in his red coat spoke English in a strange way, but Ely understood most of what he said.

"So," Dennis continued, "what is your name, young savage?"

"It is not 'young savage,'" Ely thought.

But he did not say that. He was not sure what to say. If he told them his Seneca name, they might not be able to say it. White men had a hard time speaking anything but English.

Ely put his hand on his chest. "My name," he said. "My name is Ely. It rhymes with 'freely.'"

The four white men looked surprised.

"A poet," Ralph said. "We have got us a Shakespeare in buckskins." Then he laughed. His laugh was loud and unpleasant. Something about that laugh sounded familiar to Ely. Then Ely realized why. It was like the braying of Dover, Reverend Stone's mule.

"Not likely," said the tallest of the soldiers. "Easier to make a silk purse out of a sow's ear than turn an ignorant savage into a civilized man." Then he snorted like a pig.

"Too right, Dick!" said the third man, who was as round as a barrel. "Here, here!"

Dennis raised both his hands. "Tom," he said to the round man. "Hush, now. All of you."

Tom and the other two soldiers became quiet.

"I think we have us a guide," Dennis said. "Ely, are you going this way?"

Dennis jabbed his hand toward the east.

Ely nodded. "Hamilton," he said.

Dennis grinned at his friends. "See. Our friend Ely is headed to Hamilton. Same as us."

"Whaaat?" Ralph brayed. "Do you mean to trust an Indian?"

"Do you know the way?" Dennis asked.

Ralph shook his head. He did not look happy.

"So," Dennis said, "my new friend Ely. Would you like to accompany us? Be our Native guide? Show us the way to go?"

Ely hesitated. The soldiers did not speak the way Reverend Stone spoke. They spoke English very fast and in a strange way. However, Ely was getting used to their language. And he liked this one named Dennis. Also, to help anyone who asked for help was the Seneca way.

"I . . . will . . . guide," he said.

Dennis slapped him on the back. "Good man!" he said. "Capital!"

CHAPTER SIXTEEN
Leather for Logs

At first Ely enjoyed traveling with the four English soldiers. He was not sure about Ralph, but he thought the other three liked him. They were always making jokes and laughing. At first, Ely laughed with them, though he did not understand their jokes.

But when Ely began to understand their jokes he stopped laughing. Their jokes were about him. They were making fun of him because they thought he was an ignorant savage.

"I say, Ely," Dennis said. "Tom and Dick here were at Eton, while Ralph and I are both Harrow men. Tell us where you learned that fine English you speak so well."

"Harvard, maybe," Tom snorted, a broad smile on his face.

"Public school?" Dick said.

Ralph snickered. "More likely a tavern."

The four of them laughed.

Ely looked down at the ground. He bit his lip. Did they really want him to reply?

"Come now, my boy, give us our answer," Dennis said.

"I . . . I . . . go to Tonawanda Baptist School," Ely said.

All four of the young English men roared with laughter.

"Ely," Dennis said, "Do you know how to cook?"

That was easier to answer. "Yes," Ely said.

"Capital," Dennis said. "Be a good lad and make supper for us."

That night the four Englishmen slept on one side of the fire. Ely was told to stay on the other side.

"Can you keep that fire burning all night?" Dennis asked.

"Yes," Ely replied.

"Good lad," Dennis said. He rolled over and went to sleep.

The next morning, Ely cooked breakfast for them. None of them said thank you. Instead, Dennis pointed at their packs.

"Could you carry all of those, my boy?" he said.

Ely understood what would happen if he said yes. But to say no would be lying. The packs were not that heavy. He was stronger than the four young Englishmen. They were soldiers, but they were not tough. Perhaps they would not make fun of him if he helped them carry their packs.

"Yes," Ely said.

But the second day was worse than the first.

"Strong as a horse, this one," Tom said.

"And has just about as much sense," Ralph added. "Pick up the pace, boy. Don't make me take the whip to you."

They stopped often. The four Englishmen were not strong walkers.

"Not so fast, young savage," Dick shouted at him.

"Walk at the pace of a civilized man," Tom snorted.

Ely wished he could answer them. But he did not have the words.

"I will learn English," he said to himself. "I will learn it so well that no one will ever make fun of how I speak again. I will. I will."

That evening, Ely collected wood and made a fire. He cooked dinner for the men. They took the pot from him and ate almost all of the food. They left just the scrapings for him.

"Hand me that pack, my boy," Dennis said.

"Be quick about it," Ralph said. "Lazy savage."

Dennis reached into the pack and pulled out a bottle of rum.

"All for us, lads," Dennis said, uncorking the bottle. "All for one and one for all."

"And none for our dusky young savage," Dick said.

"Who has found him a new master," Ralph chuckled as he drank from the bottle.

Ely watched as the young men drank. The Creator had told Handsome Lake that rum was an evil drink. It would make good men act bad. It would make one brother kill another.

The four Englishmen became drunk. They rolled onto their backs and looked as weak as babies.

"Boy," Ralph yelled, his voice slurred. "Get over here and pull off our boots."

"Yes," Dennis said. His voice was now as unpleasant and slurred as Ralph's. "Pull off our boots before I take a stick to you!"

"Why did I ever want to be friends with these men?" Ely thought.

As he crossed over to the other side of the fire, Ralph stuck out his foot and tried to trip Ely. Ely walked around him. He pulled off Dennis's boots. Then he did the same for the three other drunk, young Englishmen.

"Now polish those boots," Dennis said. "Do it right or I shall beat you tomorrow."

"Do it right and we will still beat you tomorrow," Dick said.

The four of them began to laugh. Those laughs turned into snores.

Ely sat by the fire for a long time. The boots he had been ordered to polish were piled in front of him. All four of the young Englishmen were sound asleep.

"Never again," he said. "Never again will anyone make fun of the way I speak."

He took out the knife that his uncle Hummingbird had given him. Its sharp edge gleamed in the firelight. He looked across the fire at the four men. They were snoring loudly. Ely stood up.

When the English officers woke at dawn, Ely was gone. The campfire was cold. Ely had piled it high before he slipped off into the night, but boots cut into pieces by a sharp knife did not burn as long as logs.

CHAPTER SEVENTEEN
Ready to Help

Ely walked faster after leaving the British soldiers. It took less than two more days to reach home. As always, his mother was waiting for him in front of their cabin. She held out her arms.

Ely's mother was a strong woman. She hugged him so tightly that it hurt his ribs. Ely did not complain. He was home at last.

His mother stepped back and looked up at him.

"You have grown more," she said.

Ely patted his stomach. "I am thinner, too," he said with a smile. "I need your good food, my mother."

His stomach did not stay empty long. Wolf Woman fed him stew and biscuits. He ate like a wolf. The more he ate, the more his mother smiled. When he was almost finished eating, he looked up.

"Where is my father?" he said.

"Your father is meeting with the other chiefs," Wolf Woman told him.

Ely nodded. He had seen the new houses the Ogden Land Company had built for white people close to the reservation. The company was still trying to take all of the Seneca land. The Seneca leaders were meeting to make plans and write more letters to Albany and Washington.

His mother looked at him. Ely thought he knew what she was thinking. She knew what he was thinking. So he said it.

"I have come back to return to school," he said. "I want to speak English and read and write as well as any white person. I want to help our people."

Wolf Woman reached out her hand and placed it on top of his. Once her hand had been bigger than his. Now it looked small on top of Ely's wide hand.

"Good," she said.

Ely looked around.

"Your brothers and your sister?" she said.

Ely nodded.

"Levi has gone to town for supplies," Wolf Woman said. "Solomon and Newt are off trying to hunt birds with their little bows." She pointed with her lips toward the small maple woods behind their house. A little smile came to her face. "Can you guess where Nic and Caroline are?"

"In school?" he said.

His mother nodded.

Ely returned to the Tonawanda Baptist School the next day. Reverend Stone was delighted to see him.

"Ely, my son," he said. "My best student! You will inspire the others."

Somehow, school was not hard now. Ely did not stay in the dormitory. He got up very early, helped around the farm, and then walked to school. It was only three miles. He'd grown used to walking longer distances at Grand River.

Ely was the first to enter the classroom every morning. He read the few books there.

When he finished reading them, he read them again.

One day Reverend Stone came into the little classroom while Ely was reading. Reverend Stone was carrying a stack of books.

"Eee-lee, my son," Reverend Stone said. "You need more to read. I have brought these from my own small library."

Ely no longer felt out of place in school. It helped that Nic and Caroline were also students. The three of them spoke English together at school and at home. At home they wrote letters to each other and read them aloud.

The other students now turned to Ely for help with spelling, math, and English. He was like a second teacher in the classroom.

Two months passed and he was asked to translate in church again. Ely stood before the congregation. He had no trouble translating English into Seneca.

After three months in the school, he was called to Reverend Stone's house. There he found not only the reverend but also his mother and father waiting for him.

"Ely," the reverend said, "I must tell you something."

"Yes sir," Ely said. Reverend Stone's face was very serious. His parents looked just as serious.

"I have spoken with your mother and father. They agree with me. You must leave our school."

"What have I done wrong?" Ely thought.

The look on Reverend Stone's face changed. It turned into a grin. Ely had never seen the reverend look so happy. His parents began smiling, too.

"Ely, my best student," the reverend said. He grasped Ely's wide shoulders. "You have been accepted at Yates Academy! A fine school. You will learn so much more there. Are you not excited?"

Ely was not sure how he felt. A new school? But he'd just returned home. He'd be going to a strange place where he knew no one. He would probably be the only Indian there. Would they make fun of him as those British soldiers did?

Ely looked at Reverend Stone. He looked at his parents. They were all happy for him.

Ely forced himself to smile. "I am excited," he said.

CHAPTER EIGHTEEN
Yates Academy

Yates Academy first opened in 1841. Ely was only one year old then. It was not far from Tonawanda. Just twenty miles northeast of the reservation.

It was close, but it seemed like another world. It was not a wooden, one-room schoolhouse like the Tonawanda Baptist School. It was a fine brick building. Ely stood in front of it, looking up at the windows, a cloth bag in his right hand.

"Can I fit in here?" he thought.

Ely was dressed as a white student might dress. He wore dark pants, a white shirt with a coat over the top, and a cloth cap. New clothes bought with some of the funds provided by the Indian Civilization Fund that had been created by the government.

He bit his lip, walked up the stone steps, and entered the building.

The hallway was empty. All of the students were in the three classrooms.

Ely was no longer wearing soft moccasins. Instead he wore a new pair of well-polished shoes. Those shoes had hard soles that echoed as he stepped onto the wooden floor.

A door opened in front of him. A short man wearing glasses on the end of his nose stepped out. The man's face was round and the look on his face was pleasant. The tie around his neck was loose. His thick brown hair was not well combed. One stray lock of hair hung down almost across his right eye. The man pushed back his glasses with one finger and combed the lock of hair back with his palm.

"Ah-hah," the man said. "Methought I heard the sound of footfalls. Just as I reached the passage about the ghost of Hamlet's father walking the battlements." He smiled and opened his arms. "And here you are. No ghost at all, but flesh and blood."

Ely almost laughed. It was not just what the man said, but the way he said it. He did not understand all of the words. But it seemed that this man was not like the British soldiers he'd met on his way home from Grand River. Everything about him seemed friendly.

Ely took off his cap. "Sir," he said, "I am Ely S. Parker."

The man chuckled. "I would have bet upon that," he said. He held up an index finger. "The first of your race to join us. Nor will you be the last, young Master Parker. I shall make sure of that."

He touched his chest. "Benjamin Wilcox," he said. "Principal of this school and one-third of its faculty. On behalf of Yates Academy, allow me to say you are most welcome."

"Thank you, sir," Ely said.

"I think you will like it here," Principal Wilcox said. "Our staff may be small, but we are all college graduates. We have taught in other schools before this, but none with such promise. We have 114 young ladies and 118 young gentlemen as students." He smiled broadly at Ely. "It's 119 now, of course."

Yates Academy, Principal Wilcox explained, was unusual. Yates was a modern school where young men and young women attended classes together. It was not like the Tonawanda Baptist School, where Bible study was as important as reading, writing, and arithmetic. Yates was nonsectarian. "Nonsectarian" meant it was not run by any church.

"But we do believe in the Golden Rule here," Principal Wilcox said. "Do unto others as you would have them do unto you. Follow that rule and all will go well for you here, Master Parker."

He pushed his glasses back on his nose with his finger and brushed his hair with his hand. "Now come with me."

They went into the classroom. What Ely saw made him feel dizzy. At the Baptist school there had been students of all ages. Some had been very young. Some had been older than

Ely. This room was filled with students of his own age.

However, all of those students were white. All of them were looking at him. Some were whispering to each other.

"It is him."

"It's the Indian."

"Is he a savage?"

"Can he speak English?"

Ely looked around the classroom. All of the young men sat to the right. Twenty of them. All of the young women sat to the left. Nineteen young women.

Their wooden desks were so new that Ely could smell the pinewood and varnish. There were books on every desk, more books than Ely had ever seen before.

There was a large desk at the front of the room with a blackboard behind it. All of the words written in white chalk on that blackboard were strange.

Shakespeare. Sonnet. Bard. Hamlet. Were those words in English? Ely felt so confused that he thought about turning around, running out of the school, and going home.

Ely bit his lip. *No, I will not run away.*

Principal Wilcox rapped twice on the desk. "Class!" he said. His voice was so loud and clear that Ely almost jumped. Principal Wilcox was small, but his voice was like thunder.

The whispering stopped. Everyone looked at the principal.

Wilcox nodded. "Young ladies and young gentlemen, lend me your ears."

Some of the students smiled when he said that.

Principal Wilcox turned toward Ely. He held a hand in front of his mouth and spoke softly so that only Ely could hear his words.

"A Shakespearean figure of speech," he whispered. "It means to listen well. I am not asking them to cut off their ears and hand them to me."

He winked at Ely. Then he turned back to the class, pushed his glasses back up on his nose, and lifted his chin. He spread out his arms.

"I am honored," he said, "to introduce your new classmate. He comes from a family of chiefs. His noble family includes the great Red Jacket and Cornplanter. One day he too may join their ranks. Young ladies, young gentlemen, allow me to present to you Master Ely S. Parker."

Principal Wilcox raised his hand and gestured toward Ely. "Now."

"Welcome, Master Parker," the entire class said as one.

CHAPTER NINETEEN
Young Moses

Ely's first day of classes was confusing. Many of the students seemed friendly. But others looked at him strangely, covered their mouths, and whispered to each other as he walked past.

He was so different from everyone else at Yates. He had cut his hair short again before coming to Yates so that he might fit in better. But no one else had hair as thick and black and straight as his. And no one else had brown skin.

"Can I ever fit in here?" Ely thought. He pushed that thought aside. *I will fit in. I will!*

He was standing in front of the dormitory where he would be staying. He held the bag with his spare clothing against his chest. He looked up the steps and bit his lip.

"Parker," someone said from behind him.

Ely turned. A short young man with big ears, a small nose, and thin blond hair was standing there.

"Harry," the young man said. His high voice sounded friendly.

"Harry," the young man said again. "Though I am not at all hairy, as you can see." He laughed at his own joke. "Harry Flagler at your service. But you may just call me Flagler. That's how we do it here at Yates. Last names first, eh? Yes, yes, that is how we do it!" He laughed again. Then he reached up to pat Ely on the shoulder. "Don't you worry, old chap. No, no. You will soon get used to this place."

Ely just stood there. Harry—or Flagler—had spoken those words so fast that he almost sounded like a chipmunk.

Flagler reached out and took Ely's bag. "Come along, Parker. Come along now. Time to show you to your room."

Harry Flagler spun around and ran up the steps.

Ely followed. He felt like a bear chasing a squirrel. But he also had a smile on his face.

"Perhaps," he said to himself, "I have found a friend."

As the days passed, Ely learned that the students at Yates did not just learn reading and writing. They studied the great writers of England. They read books by John Milton, William Shakespeare, and many others. They also talked about those books. Ely liked those discussions. He listened at first and said little. But when he did say anything, he spoke clearly and well. His new friend Harry was the first to take note of that.

"Parker," Harry said after class. "Your voice may be the finest one at Yates. When you speak, everyone listens. Indeed they do. And you make every word count. Not a wasted word. Not a wasted phrase. Yes, yes, indeed. That is certainly so. You might have a career in the law ahead of you."

Harry was in all of Ely's classes. So was another young man named Reuben Warren. Reuben was very different from Harry. While

Harry was very short and round, Reuben was tall and thin. Harry's face was shaped like the moon. Reuben's face was long and narrow. Harry talked fast and talked all the time. Reuben's voice was deep and as slow as molasses.

In other ways, those two young men were alike. They both dressed well and were not at Yates on scholarship like Ely. Reuben came from a very well-off family. So did Harry. Their lives were very different from Ely's, yet both young men seemed happy to have Ely as a friend.

Yates students had to write daily essays. At first, that was difficult for Ely. However, he developed a method. His method was this. Each day he would learn ten new words, record them in a notebook, and practice writing them. He also worked to improve his penmanship. "Penmanship" meant being able to write words clearly. He formed each letter with care, filling page after page.

He was practicing his penmanship at his desk when he felt someone looking over his shoulder. It was Reuben. Reuben touched his fingers to his forehead.

Ely did the same. It was a gesture that he and Reuben and Harry made when they saw each other. It was a sign of their friendship.

"Parker, may I?" Reuben held out his hand.

Ely handed him the page. Reuben bent over it like a heron looking for a fish. He moved his eyes slowly from top to bottom, then handed the page back.

"Perfect penmanship," he said. "Best I've seen." Then he left the room.

The students at Yates also did not do simple math of the sort Ely had learned at the Baptist school. They studied algebra and geometry. Ely was surprised at how easily he learned both subjects.

"You have a fine mind for mathematics," Principal Wilcox said to him. "Perhaps you may become an engineer."

Ely felt himself changing. English was now easy for him. Perhaps it was because everyone around him spoke English. He would never forget his Native language. He would always remember Seneca. However, English was now a part of him. He even began to dream in English.

Ely also learned other languages—Greek and Latin. Those languages were spoken long ago in Europe. Many great books were written in those old languages. Ely liked the sound of those languages and would read them aloud to feel the words on his tongue.

After his first month at Yates Academy, Ely was called to the office of the principal.

Principal Wilcox was sitting behind his desk.

"Have a seat, Master Parker."

Ely sat with his back straight and his hands on his knees. He looked Principal Wilcox in the eye.

"I called you here because I have a question for you," Wilcox said.

"Yes, sir," Ely replied.

"How do you like life at our academy?"

"I like it very well," Ely said.

Wilcox smiled. "Excellent. I have heard nothing but fine things about you. It seems you have taken to Yates as a fish takes to water."

"Thank you, sir," Ely said. He bit his lip and took a breath. "May I ask you a question?"

Principal Wilcox raised one eyebrow. "Of course, of course, Master Parker. And what might that question be?"

"The other students pay for their tuition. They pay for their room and board. Why am I given all of this for free?"

Principal Wilcox leaned back in his chair. He pushed his glasses back on his nose. Then he leaned forward and put his hands together.

"You and your people have been treated badly by white men, Master Parker," the principal said. "Your land has been taken, your ancient ways destroyed. Some say there is no hope for the Indian. Some even wish for your people to vanish from the earth. And others covet what little land is left to you. Am I correct about this?"

Ely stared at Principal Wilcox. He had never heard a white man speak that way before.

"Yes," Ely said. "That is all true."

Wilcox pressed his fingertips together. "Indeed. But not all white men are like that. Many see the Indian as a brother. An ignorant and weaker brother, to be sure, but one who is still our relative. They wish to help him. But his old ways are no longer good. He must give up those wild ways. He must learn the ways of civilization. Then he and his people may be lifted up to walk among us as equals. That is how those of us who are true Christians feel. That is why you were admitted to Yates. That is why you have also received financial support from the Indian Civilization Fund.

"You have great promise, Ely. Through the new idea of education, you may become as good as any white man. You may be as Moses in the Bible. You may be the first of your people to lead them from the wilderness of the old Indian ways to the Promised Land of modern civilization."

Ely nodded. Principal Wilcox was sincere. But gaining a white education to help his people was not a new idea. "Learn the ways of the white men," Red Jacket had said. "Do this to help your people."

"Thank you, sir," Ely said. "I shall do my best."

Principal Wilcox stood up and brushed his hand back through his hair. He smiled broadly. "I know you shall," he said. "I know you shall, young Moses."

Ely walked out into the hall. He thought about what Principal Wilcox had told him. It was good that some white men wished to help the Indian. But Ely did not think that he and his people were ignorant and weak. Nor did he wish to become as good as any white man. He believed he was already as good as any white man. He would learn white ways. But in his heart he would remain a Seneca.

"And I shall not be Moses," Ely said to himself.

Moses died before he reached the Promised Land.

CHAPTER TWENTY
New Friends and Pretty Girls

Everyone at Yates Academy noticed Ely. It was hard not to. It was not just because he was an Indian. He stood out because he was tall and broad-shouldered and walked with his back straight and his chin held high.

Ely also stood out because he worked hard. As the days and weeks and months passed, Ely became one of the best students in every class.

During his second week at Yates, Ely went with his friends to the field behind the school.

"Race?" Reuben said.

Ely nodded.

They lined up. A crowd of other students gathered to watch. Harry held up his hand.

"Are you ready?" Harry said. "Quite ready? Parker? Warren? Yes? To the chestnut tree and back? Agreed? All right. Then . . . go!"

Reuben ran faster than Ely expected. He pulled ahead until Ely began to run faster. He passed Reuben before they reached the chestnut tree, turned, ran back, and finished far ahead of his long-legged friend.

The students who'd gathered to watch were all cheering.

Reuben took his hand. "Fine run," he said, shaking his head.

Harry was jumping up and down. "Parker," he said, "Parker, Parker, Parker. Do you know what you have done? You have beaten the fastest runner at Yates."

After that, Reuben and Ely raced each other every week. Sometimes Reuben won. Ely never told Reuben that he slowed down to let him win.

Despite how well he did, Ely never bragged. He was serious about his studies, but he also liked to have fun. He was modest and never said anything unkind to anyone.

It was spring. Ely sat in the school library. A book was open on the desk in front of him, but he was not reading it.

Leaves were returning to the trees. Flocks of geese passed overhead. Ely thought about his aunt and uncle at Grand River. He had learned so much while he was in Canada. But he was also learning at Yates.

"Which do I prefer?" he thought. "The old way of living, hunting like a wolf? Or hunting for knowledge in books like a white man? I was happy outdoors. But I am also happy here."

Ely shook his head. He did not have to choose one way or the other.

"I can live the life of a white man and a Seneca," he thought.

"Parker," someone said.

He turned from the window. It was his friend Harry.

"Flagler," Ely said. He touched his forehead with his finger and Harry did the same.

"The Euglossians want you," Harry said. His voice was excited.

There were two literary societies at Yates Academy. Those societies were called the Euglossians and the Cleosophics. The best students were invited to join. Those two societies brought students together to debate and talk about literature.

"Are you sure of that?" Ely asked. "The Euglossians?"

"Yes, I am certain. Yes, indeed. I have been training myself to listen. The way you taught me. Talk less, listen more, eh? I have become quite good at it. And so I overheard the discussion between the president of the society and the vice president."

Ely bit his lip. "Am I up to this?"

Harry laughed. "Up to it? Parker, you are the best speaker I have ever heard. Your deep, full voice is perfect. No, no! Do not deny it!"

Ely tried to frown at Harry. But the frown turned into a smile. How could he not smile? This was wonderful news. The Euglossians!

Sure enough, Harry was right. The president of the Euglossians invited Ely to join their club.

Two weeks later, Ely stood at the front of the assembly hall. He rubbed his hands together and looked around. Then he placed his left hand on his chest and raised his right hand. Everyone grew silent.

"Fellow members of our society," he said, "I have been asked to speak." He paused and shook his head. "Alas," he said, "I do not know what to say."

In the front row, Harry leaned over to Reuben. "If you believe that," he whispered, "you also believe that water is not wet."

Reuben nodded his head. "True," he said.

Ely pretended to scowl down at them. He took a deep breath.

"My friends," Ely said in his deep voice, "it has been most difficult for me. I have been engaged in translating the crooked Indian language into the English and the English back into the same. Now I should like the society to release me, for I feel myself getting crazy. Those two languages are getting mixed in my head, and I can no longer speak a single word in either."

Ely raised one eyebrow. Everyone in the audience began to laugh and applaud at the same time. No one else had ever spoken so well about not being able to speak.

"Master Parker," the president of the Euglosssians shouted as he applauded, "your request is denied! You must remain a Euglossian."

The young women of Yates also admired Ely. One day, during the dining hour, he heard two young women whispering about him. They were sitting at a table thirty feet away. They were first-year students, like Ely. Their names were Clara and Emma. They did not know that he could hear as well as a wolf.

"Look at him," Clara whispered to her friend. "See how noble he looks."

"Oh, yes," Emma answered. "He is a copper-skinned Adonis."

Ely did not turn his head their way. But he smiled. He knew who Adonis was. Adonis was the most handsome young man in ancient Greece.

Ely knew he was not the most handsome young man at Yates. However, it pleased him to be talked about in that way. Especially by girls as pretty as Clara and Emma.

Other people were also talking about Ely. A meeting of the elders was held at the Tonawanda reservation. A few of the chiefs were worried that Ely's education was not a good thing.

"He is becoming a white man," they said. "He will no longer be loyal to his people."

But most of the elders were pleased. "He is learning how to speak for us," Ely's grandfather Sosehawa said.

"Sosehawa is right," Blacksmith agreed. "Hasanoanda now speaks English as well as any white man. He will help us."

Help certainly was needed. The Ogden Land Company was pushing their claim that they owned all of Tonawanda. Letters had to be written to Albany and Washington. Delegations had to be sent to the governor and the president. Someone who understood English was needed.

A few thought Hasanoanda was too young. But all agreed that no one else among them could write and speak English as well as Ely. So it was decided. They would call on Ely to write their letters in English to the white men in Albany and Washington. They would use him as their interpreter.

Ely was sitting in Latin class when Harry came in.

Harry looked at Ely. He touched his finger to his forehead, but he did not smile. There was a serious look on his round face. Harry went to the Latin teacher.

"Excuse me, sir," Harry said. "Beg pardon. I must bring Master Parker to the office."

"What is this about, Flagler?" Ely asked as they walked down the hall.

"Oh, you are in big trouble, Parker." Harry replied. "Yes, indeed. No doubt. I expect you are about to be thrown out of school for your poor scholarship."

Ely could tell Harry was teasing. "Flagler," Ely said, "You are the one in big trouble. When I see you later, I am going to give you a beating!"

That made Harry chuckle. Ely was the strongest young man in the school. But Ely never used his strength to hurt anyone.

They reached the principal's office.

"Farewell, Parker. Alas, alas. I leave you now to your awful fate," Harry said.

"Your awful fate is to be badly beaten," Ely said.

"First you must catch me," Harry replied.

The two of them smiled. They each touched their foreheads with their fingers. Then Harry walked away.

Ely knocked on the door.

"Come in."

Ely opened the door. What he saw surprised him. Someone was sitting in the visitor's chair in front of Principal Wilcox's desk. Chief Blacksmith.

Principal Wilcox stood up. He pushed his glasses back on his nose.

"Master Parker," he said, "your chief is here to speak with you about matters regarding your people."

Wilcox pulled out a pocket watch. He looked at it and nodded. "Time for our Shakespeare class. You may join us when you are done."

Principal Wilcox left the room, closing the door behind him.

Ely stood there, uncertain what to do.

"I greet you in peace, Hasanoanda," Chief Blacksmith said. "Now sit down. We must talk. This will not take long."

Ely sat. Chief Blacksmith opened a large pouch. He took out some papers. One paper had writing on it. The other pages were blank.

"This is a letter to the White Father in Washington, President Tyler," Blacksmith said. "We wrote it as best we could. But I think we did not write it well."

Ely looked at the letter. Chief Blacksmith was right. It was not written well. Words were spelled wrong. Sentences were incomplete.

Ely took a pencil from the principal's desk and a blank sheet of paper. He bit his lip. Then he wrote out a first draft. Chief Blacksmith waited patiently. Ely studied what he had written. He crossed out a few words and added others. Then he took a second sheet of paper. He picked up a pen. He wrote carefully, forming each letter perfectly as he wrote.

He gave the letter to Chief Blacksmith.

"Nya:weh, Hasanoanda," the chief said. He stood up. "Now you go back to your studies. We will call on you again. This will be your job for us."

Ely walked back to class thinking about what had just happened. A great weight had been placed on his shoulders. But he also felt like shouting in happiness. He was doing what his mother had dreamed. He was moving back and forth between the two worlds of the white man and the Senecas.

"This is the way," he thought, "that I will help my people."

CHAPTER TWENTY-ONE
Always, Just an Indian

Ely was enjoying his new role. He was being called on often to write letters for the chiefs to government men in Albany, the state capital, and to Washington.

He was also enjoying his life at Yates Academy. It now felt easy for him to move between the two worlds. He was still an Indian but seemed wholly accepted in the white man's world. Whenever he spoke, the lecture hall was filled. Whenever he took part in debates, his side always won.

It was a beautiful June morning. Ely sat in class, waiting for the teacher to arrive. As always, he was the first in class. Someone else came into the room. Clara Williams. Ely always noticed Clara. Everyone did. She was the prettiest girl in school, lively and popular. She was usually with a group of her friends.

They almost always were the last ones to arrive at class. They would come in laughing and talking.

"Why is she here so early?" Ely thought. He kept reading his book. The class had been assigned to read the play *Othello* by William Shakespeare. It was about a dark-skinned prince who married a white woman. Othello was the dark-skinned prince. Ely thought the story was a sad one.

Clara slipped into the desk next to him. It was not her desk. It was Harry's. Clara's was on the other side of the room. She leaned toward Ely.

Ely bit his lip. He could smell her perfume. Its scent was like flowers. His neck felt hot.

"Excuse me," Clara said.

Ely looked at her. For a moment he forgot how to speak. He bit his lip again.

Clara looked into his eyes. "You are such a good student." She placed her hand on his book. "This is so hard to understand. Could I ask your help?"

"Me?" Ely said. "Help you?"

Clara nodded. "Please."

"Yes," Ely said, "Yes, yes. Of course. I would be glad, delighted to assist you. Yes, indeed."

"I sound like Harry," Ely thought. But he was smiling as he thought it.

Soon they were talking about Othello. It seemed as if Clara understood it better than she said.

"I think it terrible," she said, "that Othello met such a sad end. Despite the color of his skin, he was noble and good."

In the days that followed, Ely found himself spending as much time with Clara as he did with Harry and Reuben.

"Good for you, Parker. She is quite the lovely lass," Harry said. "Yes, indeed. You are the first man here at Yates that she has chosen as a friend."

"True," Reuben said.

Ely became Clara's escort to every event at the school. They walked together to lectures and evening meetings. She took his hand as he helped her down the stairs.

They were never alone, though. That was not allowed. Although young men and young women went to school together at Yates, they never met privately.

Everyone in the school talked about their friendship. Some thought it was charming. Others did not approve. Ely heard what they whispered.

"Parker is forgetting his place," some said.

"Bright as he is, he is still just an Indian," others said.

Clara's friend Emma took her aside.

"Clara," she said, "have you heard what people are saying? You must break it off with Parker."

Clara shook her head. "Why should I listen to what others say? Ely is my friend. I shall not reject him."

As they sat side by side in the lecture hall, Clara reached over and touched his elbow.

"You are the most handsome young man in this room," she said.

Ely did not reply. But he sat up straighter in his seat and smiled.

Ely and Clara's friendship continued and grew as the school year went on. When July came, a rumor went around the school.

"Have you heard?" people said. "Parker is planning to hire a carriage."

"A carriage?"

"Yes. He plans to take Clara Williams for a ride on the Fourth of July."

"Ely Parker the Indian and beautiful Clara Williams? Wait till her parents hear about this."

Even Ely's good friends heard the rumors.

"Is it true?" Harry asked Ely. It was July third. Harry and Reuben and Ely were sitting together on the steps in front of the academy.

"What if it is?" Ely asked. "What is wrong about taking a young lady for a ride?"

"My friend," Harry said. "It would not bother me at all. No, not at all. But there are some who would be upset. Most upset. Is that not so, Reuben?"

"I suppose," Reuben said.

But Ely did not listen to their advice.

When the Fourth of July came, a crowd of students gathered in front of the academy. Their eyes were on the road that led past the school. They heard the sound of hooves and the rattle of wheels. A coach came into sight. It was a fine, open rig. The man driving it was a black man in a bright red coat. The students recognized him. His name was Thomas Smith. The coach and the horse, which he often rented out, were his.

In the back of the coach, Ely and Clara sat side by side. Clara held a bouquet of flowers in her hands. As they passed the school, Ely took off his hat and waved to the crowd.

"Fine day for a drive," he shouted.

Two days later, Ely sat again with Harry and Reuben on the school steps. Ely's shoulders were slumped. His face was grim.

"I cannot believe it," Ely finally said. "Clara has been withdrawn from school by her parents. They have taken her to Europe. Her friend Emma says that Clara will not be returning to Yates."

Harry put his hand on Ely's shoulder. "As I feared," Harry said. "Just as I feared."

Reuben said nothing. He put his hand on Ely's other shoulder.

"It does not matter how much I succeed," Ely thought. "In the eyes of the white world, I will always be just an Indian."

CHAPTER TWENTY-TWO
A Fateful Encounter

One spring afternoon in 1844, Ely was again in Albany. He and the Seneca chiefs had met with Governor Bouck of New York that morning. Bouck had been pleasant and friendly.

"Tell your chiefs," Governor Bouck said, "that I sympathize with them in their desire to save their reservation."

Before they left, Bouck had taken Ely aside.

"Young man," he said, "you have great promise. I expect to hear great things of you in the future."

The governor's words were pleasing, Ely thought. But they were not deeds.

This lovely April afternoon, there were no further meetings. The Seneca chiefs had not been interested in seeing more of the city.

So Ely was free to do as he pleased. As he walked along State Street, Ely looked down the hill to his left. Governor Bouck's mansion was down there.

"So many white men," Ely thought, "are like the governor. They speak words of support, but in the end they do nothing." Then he spotted a bookstore.

Ely rubbed his hands together. "Yes," he said to himself. He walked inside.

The smells of the leather bookbindings, the ink, and the paper were as pleasing to him as the scent of spring flowers. He thought for a moment of Clara. Then he shook his head. He needed to forget about her, forget about everything that was troubling. He found a shelf piled high with volumes in Greek and Latin. He picked up one by Cicero, the Roman orator, a copy of the *Aeneid* by Virgil, and a book called *Greek Grammar*. He had just enough money to buy all three.

A brown-haired, well-dressed white man came around the corner of the bookshelves. Ely moved aside to let him pass. The man did not go past him. He just stood there staring at Ely.

Ely nodded. "A good day to you, sir."

The man's mouth dropped open.

"Sir?" Ely said. "Are you unwell?"

The man did not answer Ely's question. Instead, he asked one of his own.

"Are you . . . are you an Indian?"

Ely understood. This white man was shocked to see an Indian in a bookstore. Probably, like most white men, he thought all Indians were savage and stupid.

"Alas," Ely said, a small smile on his face, "I must plead guilty as charged."

With a surprised look in his eyes, the man took a step toward him. It looked as if he was about to shout and grab hold of Ely.

"You speak English!" he said.

Ely held up the *Aeneid*. "Would you prefer to converse in Latin?" he asked.

A smile came to the man's face. He shook his head.

"Forgive me," the white man said. "I have forgotten my manners. I am just so terribly excited. My name is Morgan. Lewis Henry Morgan."

"Hasanoanda of the great Seneca Nation," Ely said. "My English name is Ely S. Parker. Pronounced Eee-lee to rhyme with 'freely,'" he added.

The white man grasped Ely's hand in both of his own.

"Hasanoanda, Mr. Ely Parker," Morgan said, "I cannot tell you how pleased I am to meet you. I have a deep interest in the Iroquois. In my hometown, my friends and I have formed a club. We call ourselves the Grand Order of the Iroquois. Many of us, especially myself, wish to learn all we can about the ancient and vanishing ways of your red people."

"We share a common interest," Ely said. He held up the book of Cicero's speeches. "I am interested in the ancient and vanished ways of your white people."

Morgan shook his head. Then he laughed. "Marvelous," he said.

Soon he and Ely were talking like old friends. Morgan explained that he was a lawyer, but his visit to Albany was for a different purpose. He'd come to do research in the state library, reading the Indian treaties in the files.

"I've been searching for books about the Iroquois, but all I can find are James Fenimore Cooper novels," Morgan said. "I long for a factual book about the Iroquois. I know so very little about your people."

Morgan looked at Ely. "I never dreamed I would meet an Indian such as yourself, one who speaks English perfectly and knows the ways of his people." Morgan paused. "But may I ask why you are here in our state capital?"

Ely told about the meetings with Governor Bouck. Morgan listened with fascination.

"Might I meet your uncle and the other chiefs?" Morgan asked.

Ely looked at Morgan and considered his request. Morgan seemed as sincere, direct, and clear as a child. He was interested in the Iroquois and said he respected them. Morgan was also a lawyer. Perhaps Morgan was a white man who would not just talk about helping the Senecas. A white lawyer could be a great help.

"Yes," Ely said. "I will arrange for you to meet them this evening."

Morgan clapped his hands together like a child who had just been promised candy.

"Wonderful!" Morgan said. "Wonderful!"

CHAPTER TWENTY-THREE
A New White Friend

Morgan came to their room that evening.

Ely introduced Morgan first to his grandfather.

"My grandfather's name is Sosehawa," Ely said. "He is the leader of our delegation. He is what you might call the great high priest of the entire Six Nations. He is the nephew of Red Jacket."

Morgan pointed at the silver medal that hung around Sosehawa's neck. "I believe I have seen that medal in portraits of Red Jacket. Is that the very medal that president George Washington gave to Red Jacket?"

"It is," Ely said.

Sosehawa smiled. "Is he admiring my medal?" he said in Seneca. He took the medal off and handed it to Ely. "Tell him that he can hold it and look at it."

Ely passed the silver medal to Morgan "My grandfather says that you can look at this."

Morgan's hands trembled as he held the very large medal. He looked at the side that showed the American eagle with its wings spread wide. He looked at the side that showed a white man and an Indian sharing a pipe. "George Washington '79" was engraved on the medal. Morgan handed it back carefully.

"Please tell your grandfather," Morgan said, "that I am greatly honored."

As Morgan sat with them, he explained that he and his friends had started a club modeled after the Iroquois League. They admired that league and they wanted to know more.

"I have read that your League of the Iroquois was democratic," Morgan said. "Is that so?"

"That is true," Ely replied. "Our fifty chiefs were like your senators in Washington. They represented all the people of the Iroquois nations at meetings. The Six Nations always helped each other. They sought peace but were ready to defend their people in war.

No one could defeat the Great League of the Six Nations in battle."

Ely turned to his grandfather. "This white man wishes to know more."

Sosehawa nodded. He spoke, pausing now and then for Ely to translate. He told the story of how the League came to be. He told how great its power was. When the war between the white brothers started, both sides asked the Iroquois League for help. The League could not agree which side to join. Without an agreement, there could be no decision.

"So the Great Council Fire was covered," Sosehawa said. "Our Great League did not ally itself with either the British or the Americans."

Sosehawa paused. "Our new friend listens with his mouth closed," he said.

"Yes, grandfather," Ely said.

Sosehawa pointed with his lips at Morgan. "Are you sure he is a white man? Most white men are all mouth. They try to do all the talking when they meet with us. This man actually seems to have two ears."

"That is true," Ely said, trying not to laugh.

"What did your grandfather say?" Morgan asked.

"He said you are a good listener."

"Please ask him to continue," Morgan said.

Sosehawa went on, telling how things went during the American Revolution. Some Iroquois joined the British. Some joined the Americans. In the battles that followed, Iroquois men fought and killed each other. The union of the Great League was broken.

After the Americans won the war, they forced the chiefs to sign a new treaty. Even the Iroquois who fought for the Americans lost most of their land. All they had left were several small reservations.

It was promised that those reservations would be theirs forever. But now the Ogden Land Company was trying to take the Seneca lands.

Morgan sat nodding his head after Ely finished translating his grandfather's words.

"I am so sorry," Morgan said. "It is wrong that the land company wants to take your land.

I am a lawyer, and I believe in law and justice for both the white man and the Indian."

Morgan paused and took a breath. "May I, may I . . . meet with you again?"

As Ely translated Morgan's words, Sosehawa and the two lesser chiefs looked at each other. Ely saw that they were thinking the same thing that he was thinking. A sympathetic white man who was a lawyer could be a useful friend.

CHAPTER TWENTY-FOUR
Rising Up the Rainbow

Ely returned to Yates after his meeting with the Seneca chiefs and the governor. His life was taking some exciting turns, but still he felt sad.

Ely sat alone in the classroom. He dipped his pen in the inkwell. He looked at the sheet of paper on his desk.

"Dear Clara," he wrote. Then he stopped. He shook his head. He put down the pen. He picked up the piece of paper. He looked at his own neat, clear handwriting. Then he folded the paper in half, folded it again, and placed it in his pocket.

Clara was gone. His missed her smile. He missed her voice and her quick intelligence. But he would not see her again. She would never return to Yates Academy. Her parents would not allow that. It was a month now since she had been taken from school. She was somewhere in Europe with her parents. Any letter he wrote would not reach her.

He thought about what his friends had said to him.

"Parker," Harry had said. "You have the finest mind of anyone I know. Yes, yes indeed. I think you are as good as any white man. But that is not how some others see you. No, not at all. They only see the color of your skin. When you went for that ride with Clara, they thought you were not staying in your proper place. You were rising above your station. It damaged Clara's reputation to be seen as your friend. Reputation means everything to some people."

"Sad but true," Reuben had added.

Sometimes people whispered as he passed.

"Such a shame about poor Clara."

"How could Parker be so foolish?"

"How could Parker dare to rise above his station that way?"

"He may be bright, but he is still just an Indian."

He ignored the whispers he overheard. He still went to every class. He was still an excellent student. He still was the best debater. He still gave talks that everyone attended. But his heart was broken.

He thought of the black wolf. He felt like that wolf. He was alone in the world with no companion.

"Parker?"

Ely turned in his chair. Reuben was standing in the doorway of the classroom. He held out a letter.

"For you," Reuben said. "From a Mr. Morgan."

Ely opened the letter and smiled as he read it.

My dear Hasanoanda,

I am delighted to tell you that the fellow members of our Society have granted you honorary membership in our Grand Order of the Iroquois. They would be most honored to have you as our guest at the annual meeting of our society in Aurora, New York.

The meeting was scheduled for the end of that month. Ely felt his heart beating faster.

"Yes," he said to himself. "This is just what I need. I need to be someplace where people are not whispering about me behind my back. It may even help me take my mind off Clara."

He took out a fresh sheet of paper. He picked up his pen and dipped it into the inkwell.

My dear Mr. Morgan,
Thank you for accepting me into your society. I would be delighted to attend the annual meeting.

Ely traveled to Aurora by coach. Morgan had sent money to pay for his travel. As the coach went down the hill into the town of Aurora, Ely saw the blue waters of Cayuga

Lake. The air smelled fresh and sweet. He could not stop smiling. Morgan was waiting for him at the coach stop.

"Hasanoanda," he said, grasping Ely's hand. "I cannot express how pleased I am that you are here."

"Thank you, my friend," Ely replied. His voice was steady, but he was as excited as Morgan. "I am just as pleased to be here."

Ely was dressed in the clothing he wore to school. However, he carried a bag with him.

"Is there somewhere I might change my clothes before the meeting?" Ely asked.

Morgan took Ely to his own home. He introduced Ely to his family.

"This is my Seneca friend of whom I have spoken so often. He is Hasanoanda, a young man from a great family. He is surely destined to be a chief of his people."

Then Morgan showed Ely to the guest room.

"I shall leave you to get ready," Morgan said.

When Ely came out of the room, he was wearing the clothes he brought with him in the bag. He wore moccasins and a loincloth. A woven belt was tied about his waist and other belts crossed over his broad, bare chest. He wore a feathered cap. He also had on the Red Jacket medal his grandfather had loaned him.

"Father, Father!" Morgan's children shouted. "Your friend has turned into an Indian."

Morgan looked embarrassed.

But Ely laughed. "It is all right," he said. "I am sure that this is what the members of your club wish to see."

Morgan smiled. "Yes," he said. "Yes, that is so."

Indeed, the members of Morgan's club were delighted.

"He is a real Indian," one man said in an awed voice.

"A true Iroquois!" another agreed.

The members of the club were even more impressed when Ely spoke. His voice was powerful, his words clear.

"I am Hasanoanda of the Haudenosaunee Nation," Ely began, "I stand before you as a representative of our Great League. We were here before your country existed. When your ancestors arrived and they were weak, we fed them and helped them survive. My ancestors fought by your side against your enemies. Now we are weak and you are strong. We seek only to survive on our own land. Will you now help us as my ancestors helped yours?"

When Ely finished his speech, there was silence for a moment. Then Morgan rose to his feet, as did all the others. They began to applaud.

"Bravo," they shouted. "Bravo!"

The next day, Morgan walked Ely to his coach.

"Hasanoanda," Morgan said, "may I come and visit you at your home?"

Ely hardly knew what to say. No white person before this had ever asked to come to his home. Even his friends Reuben and Harry had never asked to visit him. But Morgan and his club had treated Ely like a prince.

"I will ask my family," Ely said.

"Thank you, my friend," Morgan said, shaking Ely's hand. "Thank you so very much. Or, as your people say, Nya . . . nya:weh. Is that right?"

Ely smiled. "Yes," he said. "Nya:weh, my friend."

As soon as Ely reached Yates, he wrote a letter to his brother Nic. He asked if their mother and father would accept a visit from Ely's white friend.

Nic's reply came back right away.

My dear brother,
Our parents would be most delighted to have Mr. Morgan visit. Please assure him that, humble though it may be, Mr. Morgan may think of our home as his own.

Ely sat at his desk reading Nic's letter. It was good news. It was not like the other letter he had received that day from the Indian Civilization Fund.

Ely walked to the window. It was a beautiful day. His friends were out there. So were the other Yates students and the three teachers. They were all walking around and talking with each other. Everyone looked happy and carefree. Only Ely was still inside.

Harry turned and looked Ely's way. He waved for Ely to come out.

Ely waved back and shook his head.

I am a stranger here. I am an Indian.

Morgan and his club admired him. But most white people did not admire Indians. Indians were less than white men. He had thought it was different at Yates. At first, he had been treated with respect by his teachers and fellow students. But when he made friends with a white girl, that had changed.

Clara, I still miss you. I am sorry for the trouble I caused you.

It would be so much easier to just go home and just be an Indian again. He could help his family by working on their farm. The Ogden Land Company was now sending rough white men to cut down their trees. Some of them came armed with clubs and tried to drive people from their homes.

"I could help fight them," Ely thought. He pictured himself standing by the side of his brothers against the Ogden ruffians.

Ely shook his head. "No, I must not do that now. I must remain here as long as I can. I came here to become better educated. I can use that education to help my people. They need my help in Albany and Washington to fight the Ogden Land Company."

Ely bit his lip. "But how long can I remain here?" he thought.

Ely turned away from the window. He sat down again at the desk. He picked up the second letter that contained the bad news from the Indian Civilization Fund. Ely would not be receiving any more money to pay for his schooling.

When the time finally came for Morgan to visit, Ely arranged to leave school and be at home to meet him.

"What you see here," Ely said to Morgan, "is a real place. It is far different from the novels of James Fenimore Cooper. The five hundred Indians who live here at Tonawanda are mostly farmers growing corn, oats, barley, and wheat. Our people do not make their living as hunters and trappers. Instead of hunting, we have cattle, hogs, and sheep. Most of our forestlands are gone. What woods remain are being logged to provide timber, hemlock bark, and firewood. We have no longhouses. Our people live in log cabins and frame houses."

"I see," Morgan said. But he did not seem disappointed.

Ely's parents, along with his brothers and sisters, welcomed their son's white friend. Wolf Woman fed him corn soup and venison steak. She told Morgan about the dream she had before Ely was born.

Morgan nodded his head as Ely translated his mother's words.

"Her dream is coming true, my dear friend," Morgan said. "You are rising up that rainbow. You are on your way to becoming great in both the world of my people and your own."

Dragonfly was quieter than his wife. But he showed Morgan things. He had built a small model of a longhouse so that Morgan could see the way the Senecas used to live.

Made of bent sticks and covered with elm bark shingles, the little model had an open doorway at either end. Morgan looked inside.

"Our old longhouses," Ely said, "were much bigger. Either that or my ancestors were much smaller."

He and Morgan both laughed at the joke.

"Seriously, my friend," Morgan said, "how large were these dwellings?"

"Very large indeed," Ely replied. "Some of them were as much as forty feet wide and two hundred feet long."

Morgan's stay lasted several days. On the third day of his visit, Ely and his father took Morgan to a condolence ceremony.

Morgan was in awe as the ceremony took place. Ely explained it all to him in a quiet voice.

"This ceremony is for one of our chiefs who died. A new chief, selected by the women of his clan, is now taking his place. That new chief is being given the name that the old chief held."

"Shall it be that way for you one day?" Morgan asked. "Will you become a chief that way?"

Ely shook his head. "I cannot say. It is only the women of the clan who decide."

After the ceremony, Morgan grasped Ely's arm.

"Hasanoanda, my dear friend," Morgan said. "If I were to write a book about your people, would you help me?"

"Yes," Ely said. But he looked worried.

"What is wrong?" Morgan said. "Have I asked too much?"

Ely shook his head. "The Indian Civilization Fund has denied my request for further funds for my education. I shall have to leave Yates Academy."

To Ely's surprise, a broad smile came over Morgan's face. Morgan clapped his hands together. "Wonderful!" Morgan said. "Wonderful."

Ely was confused.

"Why is my friend glad that I shall have to leave school?" he thought.

Morgan saw the confused look on Ely's face.

"Hasanoanda," Morgan said, "It is time for you to leave Yates. There is a far better school for you to attend. Cayuga Academy. And I have spoken with the other members of our Grand Order. They have agreed to sponsor you. We would pay all of your expenses."

Ely looked at the ground.

Morgan clapped his hands together. "My friend," he said, "please tell me that you will accept our offer."

Ely lifted his head. His heart felt full.

"My friend," Ely said, "if I go to this school, can I still help you?"

Morgan laughed. "Hasanoanda, my dear friend, I have no intention of losing you. Cayuga Academy is not just a fine school, it is in Aurora, my own hometown. We can see each other often."

Morgan placed his hands on Ely's shoulder. "Cayuga is the same school that I attended. It prepared me to be a lawyer and can do the same for you. Cayuga Academy could carry you even farther up that rainbow of your mother's dream. I see a future for you in the practice of law. Think of that! An Indian lawyer!"

A lawyer, Yes! I could do even more to help my people as an Indian lawyer.

Ely smiled so broadly he thought his face would split. His mother's dream was being fulfilled. He could feel his rainbow rising above him. "Nya:weh, my friend," he said. "I accept."

Afterword

Ely Parker was an excellent student at Cayuga Academy, but his stay there was brief. He had to leave Cayuga Academy in 1847 after only one semester. He was called upon by his people to go with a delegation to Washington, DC. It was led by Chief Blacksmith, whose title was Donehogawa, "Keeper of the Western Door." For several years after that, Ely traveled back and forth to Washington for the Tonawanda Senecas. He also continued to work with Lewis Henry Morgan and was a source of information about the Iroquois for such famous writers as Henry Schoolcraft.

During that time, he was accepted as a student of law in the office of William P. Angel, a lawyer who was a district attorney and a federal Indian agent. However, Ely's career in law ended after a year of study. Under New York law, only a natural born or a naturalized citizen could be admitted as a lawyer. American Indians were not citizens, and Ely was refused admission. In 1849, he turned to a career in engineering. He began working for the state of New York on the New York State canals.

In 1851, Lewis Henry Morgan published *League of the Ho-de-no-sau-nee*, or Iroquois, and dedicated it as follows: "To Ha-sa-no-an-da (Ely S. Parker)" as "the fruit of our joint researches."

In 1851, after the death of John Blacksmith, a condolence ceremony and grand council of the Six Nations was held. At that ceremony, Ely Parker was given the title of Donehogawa. At the age of twenty-three he had become, as he now signed his letters, "Grand Sachem of the Six Nations of Indians in New York and Canada." He was also formally given the Red Jacket medal at that same ceremony.

Over the next several years, Ely represented the Tonawanda Senecas in Albany and Washington and at meetings with Presidents Polk, Taylor, Fillmore, and Pierce.

He was also active in the local volunteer militia (the equivalent of the modern National Guard), where he earned the rank of captain of engineers in the 54th Regiment of the New York state militia.

In 1857, the U.S. Supreme Court ruled that the Ogden Land Company could not remove the Tonawanda Senecas from their land. The ruling was followed by a new treaty in 1858 that allowed the Tonawanda Senecas to keep more than half of their land.

While living in Galena, Illinois, Ely met a former army officer who had served in the Mexican War. That officer was now working in a store owned by his wife's father. The two men became close friends. The former army officer, who returned to the army when the Civil War started, was none other than Ulysses S. Grant. Grant became a general and commander of the Union soldiers and president after the war.

Ely tried to volunteer for the Union army. He knew that engineers were needed. But he was turned down each time he tried. He even approached William Seward, the secretary of state, a fellow New Yorker who knew Ely well. Again, he was refused because he was an Indian. "The fight," Seward told him, "was an affair between white men and one in which the Indian was not called on to act."

However, in 1863, Ely's friends in the army acted on his behalf. He was appointed to be an important administrative officer in the Union army. He went on to become Grant's personal secretary and was by Grant's side for the rest of the war. When the war ended at Appomattox, it was Ely who wrote out the terms of the surrender of the Army of Virginia. General Robert E. Lee, the commander of the Southern forces, said to Ely as he shook his hand, "I am glad to see one real American here." Ely's gracious reply was, "We are all Americans."

About the Author

Joseph Bruchac is a writer and traditional storyteller whose work often reflects his American Indian (Abenaki) ancestry and the Adirondack Region of northern New York where he lives in the house that he was raised in by his grandparents. He holds a B.A. in English from Cornell University, an M.A. in Literature and Creative Writing from Syracuse and a Ph.D. in Comparative Literature from the Union Institute of Ohio. He is the Founder and Executive Director of the Greenfield Review Literary Center and The Greenfield Review Press.

A martial arts expert, he holds a 5th degree black belt and Master's rank in Pentjak-silat and in 2014 earned a purple belt in Brazilian jiu jitsu. He and his two grown sons, James and Jesse, who are also storytellers and writers, work together in projects involving the preservation of Native culture, Native language renewal, teaching traditional Native skills and environmental education.

Author of over 120 books in several genres for young readers and adults, his experiences include running a college program in a maximum security prison and teaching in West Africa. His newest books include a picture book co-authored with his son James, RABBIT'S SNOW DANCE (Dial), a bilingual collection of poems in English and Abenaki co-authored by him and his younger son Jesse, NISNOL SIBOAL/TWO RIVERS (Bowman Books), and the young adult post-apocalyptic novel KILLER OF ENEMIES (Tu Books), winner of the 2014 Native American Librarians Association Award.

PathFinders novels offer exciting contemporary and historical stories featuring Native teens and written by Native authors.

For more information, visit:
NativeVoicesBooks.com

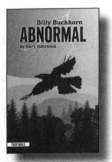

Billy Buckhorn: Abnormal
Gary Robinson
978-939053-07-7 • $9.95

Son Who Returns
Gary Robinson
978-1-939053-04-6 • $9.95

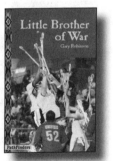

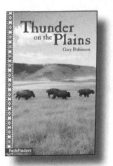

Little Brother of War
Gary Robinson
978-1-939053-02-2 • $9.95

Thunder on the Plains
Gary Robinson
978-1-939053-00-8 • $9.95

Available from your local bookstore or you can buy them directly from:

Book Publishing Company • P.O. Box 99 • Summertown, TN 38483
888-260-8458

Please include $3.95 per book for shipping and handling.

PathFinders novels offer exciting
and historical stories featur...
written by Native autho...

DA

No Nam

No Name
Tim Tingle
978-1-939053-06-0 • $9.95

Tribal Journ...
Gary Robinson
978-1-939053-01-5 • $9.95

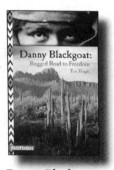

**Danny Blackgoat,
Navajo Prisoner**
Tim Tingle
978-1-939053-03-9 • $9.95

**Danny Blackgoat:
Rugged Road to Freedom**
Tim Tingle
978-1-939053-05-3 • $9.95

Available from your local bookstore or you can buy them directly from:

Book Publishing Company • P.O. Box 99 • Summertown, TN 38483
888-260-8458

Please include $3.95 per book for shipping and handling.